To, Rena w

UNFAILING LOVE

A Sequel to *Love Never Fails*

Samantha Arran

ARTHUR H. STOCKWELL LTD
Torrs Park   Ilfracombe   Devon
Established 1898
www.ahstockwell.co.uk

British Library Cataloguing-in-Publication Data.
A catalogue record for this book is available
from the British Library.

This is an entirely fictional story,
and no conscious attempt has been made
to accurately record or recreate
any real-life events.

By the same author:
Love Never Fails
Jason and Marigold

To Stephen, thanking you for your love, kindness and help; also for always being such a good friend and son. I am very proud of you and the way you have coped, and cope, with your illness.

Proceeds from this book, as from *Love Never Fails*, will be given to chosen charities.

I would like to thank everyone who has encouraged me, especially my 'baby sister', Marie, who has waited for this sequel with great eagerness.

ISBN 978-0-7223-3962-6
Printed in Great Britain by
Arthur H. Stockwell Ltd
Torrs Park   Ilfracombe
Devon

List of Characters

Amanda and Mark's children:
Twins: Vincent and Holly, 7 years.
Triplets: Eric, Heather and Sophie, 5 years.
Luca, 3 months.

Amanda's family in London:
Father: Lord Justice Jonathan Dansie.
Mother: Lady Teresa.
Brother: Joshua (Josh), lawyer.
Sister-in-law: Nicola (Nicci), fashion co-editor.
Joshua and Nicola's children:
Rose, 16 years, aspiring ballet dancer.
Twins: David and Andrew, 13 years.
Susan, 11 years.

Mark's family:
Father: former Chief Inspector Stan Young.
Mother: Isabel.
Brothers: Luke, police fitness instructor.
Adam.

Precious friends, part of family:
Former Chief Inspector Hawkins (Bob).
Reverend Matthew, vicar of The Open Church.
Count Luca, Amanda's business associate, and his sons Lorenzo and Santorini.
Joan, former nanny and dearest friend.
Lord Richard, financial advisor, his wife Sarah, and babyAngela.

Chapter 1

Adam came home from Cambridge for the Easter holidays. The local police still hadn't a vacancy where he would use all his university-masters-degree qualifications in business studies and economics. He had applied two years before for when he had completed his studies. There was an opportunity to apply for a position in Cambridgeshire early the following year. They promised to contact him with this and any other vacancy they heard about. Adam thanked them and enquired what the job would entail, and he was disappointed when they told him it wouldn't require him to use all his skills.

After Adam talked with his father, brothers and Amanda, they told him that whatever he decided it was his life and they would all support him. They suggested he should have a gap year and he agreed.

"Perhaps you need to be thinking of looking at vacancies in local businesses," Amanda suggested.

"Yes, thank you, Amanda, but I have always wanted to work in the police – with Dad and my brothers being in the force. But I realise I mustn't put all my eggs in one basket."

Amanda asked, "What does this mean? Are you going to look around?"

"Yes," laughed Stan.

They all joined in laughing. Amanda was still learning Adam's sayings.

"One option to consider is setting up your own graphics business. Then you would use your administration skills as well as your creative flair."

Adam had gained a masters degree in art, design and computer graphics between passing his degree in business studies and beginning his three-year masters course in business studies and economics.

"Thank you, Mark; that is certainly something to think about. I now have my money from our home."

"It's good you are having a gap year, Adam. There are all kinds of possibilities for your career," his father advised him.

"Yes – thanks, Dad."

Mark agreed: "You have worked hard, Adam, through your schooling and university."

They all smiled at him.

When Knutts, a very prestigious graphics business, heard on the grapevine about Adam having a gap year, they approached him to ask if he would help them to design birthday and Christmas cards, also calendars. Their office was within a short travelling distance of Chiverton. Adam accepted, and, from the money his father had invested for him when their home was sold, he bought a car.

He went from strength to strength at Knutts, and he was approached to design book covers. Ryman's, the cards manufacturer, asked if he would design special Christmas cards for relatives for them.

He was very thankful to have this work, but he realised that, although he loved the work, it wasn't fulfilling enough for him. He hoped eventually to get married. He had girlfriends, but that's all they were. He began to think that perhaps he should branch out on his own, combining art and his business expertise. He shared his thoughts with his father, brothers and Amanda. They knew he was mature enough to take this project on, and they prayed about it.

Stan had inherited his parents' home and investments before Luke and Adam were born, and, after the sale of this home, he and Isabel had bought The Laurels, a manor house in its own grounds. With him, Luke and Adam now living at Chiverton, he sold it and split the money with Isabel. He divided his share among his three sons.

A few days after the discussion with Adam, Mark spotted a unit in a new block of offices up for sale. He made a mental note of the estate agent's number and he later rang them asking for details. They knew from his voice that it was the Chief Superintendent. He texted Adam to tell him what he had done. Adam thanked him.

Adam and Stan went to view with the estate agent, Mr Sandford. The rooms were large and the windows allowed plenty of light to come through. There were good parking facilities. It had every potential.

Temporary stenographers were using the office. The manager, Mr Lee, told Adam and Stan that because of the recession full-time office staff had been made redundant and replaced with these stenographers. Their business had grown so they were moving to larger premises. The stenographers didn't stop working whilst Adam and Stan were there; Adam was very impressed – especially with a fair, curly-haired young lady.

Adam thanked the estate agent and told him he would let him know what he decided to do.

"I must warn you, we have had a lot of interest. I know this is agent's jargon, but, with your family, I wouldn't dare to try to pull the wool over your eyes."

Adam and Stan laughed, shook Mr Sandford's hand and went outside.

"As you know, Dad, I haven't enough money for this, but I will be able to take a mortgage out."

"No, Adam, there is no need for that. Mark is settled and Luke has his fitness-training business. I will tell them that I am helping you out."

"Thanks for that, Dad." He hugged his father.

When Stan told Mark and Luke, they approved of him helping.

"He is our baby brother!" Mark said with a laugh.

Adam was in constant touch with his mother, whereas Mark and Luke were polite but distant. He rang her and told her of this new beginning.

"Have you enough money, darling?"

"No, Mum, but I have my share from our home and the trust fund you and Dad set up when I was born. I will be OK. Mark and Luke have approved of Dad helping me set up."

"Darling Adam, there is no need for this! Please allow me to help you. I will make arrangements to now divide my share of our home with my three boys. You would receive this money when I die anyway. Please use it whilst I am alive. I have always felt guilty about taking this money. David will agree with me – we are very comfortable. Adam, may I talk with you?"

"Yes, of course, Mum. Thank you for the money. I will make sure my new venture will flourish. I am proud of you, Mum."

Isabel was crying. "How can you say that when I left you when you were so young?"

"I mean it, Mum. It wasn't right, but that's life."

Isabel recognised a new maturity in her baby.

"But we have moved forward," Adam continued. "We are very God-blessed to have Amanda and live at Chiverton as part of her family. You are now happy again with David."

"Yes, darling, this is what I need to talk to you about. Will it upset you if I tell you we would like to marry?"

"I will be very happy if you do, Mum. Congratulations to you and David!"

"Will you come over for the wedding – just a quiet ceremony – and give me away, Adam? Perhaps Lady Amanda will be unable to travel, but may I ask you to tell her and Mark that they will be welcome. I hope Luke will also come with you."

"I'll tell them, Mum, and I will be happy to give you away."

He put his phone down and started crying. He couldn't help it.

He went and freshened up, found his father and told him of the conversation. Stan was pleased that Isabel had generously offered to divide her share among her three sons. He knew she hadn't been selfish and greedy for money. He had mixed emotions about her remarrying. He had been expecting it and really preferred this to her and David living together.

Stan and Adam went for a walk. They didn't talk; they were both busy with their own thoughts. When they met up with Amanda, Mark and Luke, Adam asked if he could have a talk with them.

They cleared a space and Adam told them about his telephone conversation with Isabel. They were all touched by her generosity in releasing her share to them.

"I appreciated you, Dad, offering to help me buy this unit, but now Mum is giving me money I will have more than enough. I feel this is only fair to my brothers."

Mark and Luke protested, but Adam was firm and they all admired him for his unselfish thinking.

A pang went through Amanda as she thought, 'Isabel must have been a good mother whilst they were growing up, teaching them Christian principles. What a shock it must have been when they knew she was leaving them! How would her father, Josh and she have coped if Teresa had left them for another man?'

She voiced her thoughts and ended with, "We have each other now, but the children have a right to see Isabel occasionally. We will be able to explain the situation when they are a little older. Just now they still accept she lives in Spain."

Luke said, "They must wonder. They are intelligent, Amanda."

"Yes, but unless they question, perhaps we should leave well alone."

They all agreed.

"Their classmates have grandparents and parents who have separated," Mark told them.

Amanda was getting depressed thinking how she had added to Mark's burden by her carrying unforgiveness for him when Andrew, her fiancé, had been killed in Afghanistan. She knew Mark must have been deeply hurt at the time by her cruel accusations of neglect. How would she have felt if she had been so accused by the bereaved of the members of her team after they were unexpectedly attacked and killed? She groaned.

Mark thought the atmosphere was getting too heavy, so to lighten it he told Amanda, "If you ever think of leaving me, I will handcuff you."

Amanda realised what he was doing, so she jested, "Oh yes – you and whose army?" The tenseness then left.

They went quiet when Adam told them of Isabel remarrying and asking him to give her away. Luke immediately said he would go with him to the wedding.

"It's awkward for us to go to Spain with Amanda feeding Luca," Mark thoughtfully said.

Stan agreed.

Amanda suggested they buy them a wedding present.

Stan thanked her. "That will be enough, Amanda, you are very generous in allowing her to come to visit her grandchildren. What will we do after they are married? Is it right to now invite David?"

"I think so, Dad," Amanda replied. "Not to stay here, but for the day!"

Mark gathered her close. "Thank you, precious Amanda, you are a star," he said.

Adam and Luke cuddled her.

"Adam and I will never marry," Luke told her. "You are the most, Amanda! Besides, we are so comfortable here. What a shame you didn't have any sisters!"

They all laughed. The tension lifted.

"You understand I will need to go out for that day," Stan said.

"Of course we do, Dad. You do what you are comfortable with," Mark told him.

Luke and Adam agreed also. Stan had gone out with his pals on other occasions when Isabel had visited.

Amanda left them on their own to talk.

"This unit, Adam, is it big enough for you? Now you have more money, you could have something bigger."

"Thanks, Mark, but it's big enough for a start. It's on the ground floor, full of light, and has good private parking facilities. Also it's near to Chiverton and accessible for me to visit customers and them to visit me. If possible, I would like all of us to visit it before I finally accept."

Adam made an appointment with Lord Richard, Amanda and Mark's financial advisor. After studying the papers, Lord Richard gave his approval.

"Better to invest in bricks than shares," he advised.

Adam arranged to meet the estate agent again.

Amanda explained to the children: "I have to go out this lunchtime to help Uncle Adam."

They accepted this. Amanda was again surprised by their maturity – they were growing up too fast.

Vincent told her, "We understand, Mum: you have commitments. We will be OK."

"You have to work round Luca's feed, Mum," Holly said.

Amanda gathered her children up and cuddled them. "You are growing up too fast," she said. "I suppose I will not be allowed to cuddle you soon!" She laughed.

"You will, Mummy," they all assured her.

Eric asked her, "Please not in front of our friends, Mummy!"

"OK, fair enough."

"Will Granddad and Nanny Joan fetch us?"

"No, Uncle Bob will come with Nanny; Granddad will be with us."

They examined the unit with all their intelligence. They saw the survey: 100% satisfactory. The unit was only four years old. It had under-floor heating, a small kitchen, a shower room with a toilet, and a separate toilet. The block was situated in a prestigious residential area. When they had all agreed it was satisfactory for his needs, Adam rang his mother and asked her permission.

"Darling, the money is yours – you don't have to ask me."

Adam asked Mr Sandford to draw up the contract.

Mr Lee gave them his business card and told them to call him if they needed his help at any time.

Amanda told him she hired a stenographer at times, but she was very happy with the agency she used. However, she said she would bear him in mind.

He thanked her.

Travelling back, Adam said, "I most probably will need a stenographer for a few hours to help me get set up. Are you able to get a profile of the staff, Mark?"

Mark assured him he would do that.

Luke in an innocent voice enquired, "Is there anyone who caught your eye, Adam?"

"Well, the young lady with the long curly hair looked very efficient."

Luke laughed to himself. He had seen how Adam's eyes had kept wandering in her direction.

"They all looked very efficient," Amanda said with a laugh.

The police all knew about Mr and Mrs Land being transferred from near Huddersfield to update some well-known food stores in

Brookwell and the surrounding area. Their daughter Hilary had recently come home to them after completing her studies of languages, and she was now a qualified stenographer.

"Adam, it would be wiser at first for you to have a male stenographer with your being on your own," Amanda advised him.

"You are right, Amanda. I understand your concern. I will be careful not to get into any compromising situations."

"Thank you, darling."

They were all impressed again by Adam's maturity.

"We now have to stop thinking of you as our baby brother, Adam, and respect you as a man who is going to run his own business," said Mark.

They all agreed.

"You know we will always be there for you," Mark told him.

Adam thanked them again.

"Also, Adam, your administration skills will now be used," Amanda reminded him.

"Yes, I thought of that, Amanda. Thank you."

Amanda told Mark what the children had asked about not cuddling them in front of their friends. "They are growing up too fast," she said.

Mark agreed with her.

They got back to Chiverton in time to see the children before Bob and Joan took them to school. Mark's assistant picked him up and Amanda went upstairs to feed Luca.

When Adam and the estate agent returned to the unit the next lunchtime, Hilary was getting her bicycle.

Adam said, "Good morning."

She smilingly replied, "Good morning, Mr Young."

He asked, "Do you like to cycle?"

"Yes, I try to keep fit – especially after sitting at the computer."

"There are a group of us who go cycling in the evening; perhaps you would like to join us sometime?"

"Thank you – I would love to. I am new here and don't know anyone apart from the people at the local Fellowship. My parents have moved here. My name is Hilary Land.

"My friends and I are meeting at our local gym this evening. You would be welcome to join us."

"Thank you – I will."

"Right – 8 it is, then. How will you get there?"

"I will cycle," she laughed.

She rode off. He was overwhelmed he had had the nerve to ask her.

When he told his family, Luke teased him, "I had better be there this evening to make sure everything's satisfactory." (Luke owned the gym.)

Adam laughed; he knew Luke was teasing him.

When Hilary told her parents she was going to the local gym, they were surprised. Her mother asked, "Are you going on your own, Hilary?"

"No. I have been invited by Mr Young to meet him and his friends."

Her father said, "He owns the place."

Hilary was surprised. "He is buying the unit where we work," she said.

Her father was surprised again. "He is a policeman," he told her.

She laughed. "Oh, Dad, the Mr Young I am going with is an administrator and artist."

"Sorry, darling, I must be thinking of his older brother."

Her parents were very pleased she was making friends. They had been worried that she would find it hard to settle with them away from her friends near Huddersfield.

Chapter 2

Count Luca Villani faxed Amanda: "Darling, I need to see you. May I come very soon?"

She rang him on her secure line, and they conversed in Italian.

"You will be very welcome as always, Luca. When are you able to come? I will try to work round this."

He asked, "Is Wednesday morning convenient, darling Amanda?"

"Of course! I will clear this. Will you be able to stay for lunch?"

"Yes please. We need to discuss our shipping business."

Amanda had been expecting this. She knew that two of the ships were docked for major repairs. The ships were Luca's babies. He now had five, but they were wearing out. Amanda had inherited her Aunt Sophie's 20% share in this business. She thought the ships needed a lot of money to be spent on them.

"As you know, Amanda darling, our airline business is thriving – we cannot accommodate all the requests. We now have an opportunity of expanding. Sergio Rossi is selling up his airline and he has given us the first opportunity to buy. He is only fifty-four, but he has decided to retire after working hard all his life. He has even been too busy to marry. He is going to go on cruises and see the world."

Amanda understood this. She had heard of Sergio Rossi and how committed he had been to his business. When her aunt died, Amanda had also inherited major shares in an airline run by Luca and his sons.

Luca put her fully in the picture about his ships and the money they needed spending on them. "We need to consider selling this business, Amanda," he said. "Please think about this and also about

14

buying Sergio's airline. There is big money in airlines these days. Are you willing to come into this new venture with us with a 40% share? You no doubt need to discuss this with Mark."

"Yes, darling, I do. I also need to have the full details. How much do you hope I will invest with you?"

He told her, "There will be money from the ships – if we agree to sell, of course. Not as much as if they were in tip-top condition, but should we spend vast amounts building these up or buy Sergio's airline?"

"We need to look fully into this, darling Luca; will you set up a business meeting? With my feeding Luca, is it possible for Santorini and Lorenzo and everyone else to come here?"

"It is, darling. When would be your best time and day?"

"I'll check my diary. One morning after my swimming therapy would suit me best, or for once the children could be occupied if afternoon would suit everyone else better."

"Leave this with me, darling."

The meeting was set up for the next Friday morning, which was convenient for everyone. Amanda asked Mark if he would attend.

He explained: "It would be awkward for me to have time off, and it isn't necessary for me to be there. I will pull out all the stops to have lunch with you, sweetheart."

The Morley chefs were fully booked with a wedding reception, so Amanda hired an agency chef to help her own chef, Gerald. She also hired waiters from the Devonshire.

Amanda didn't have her swimming therapy that morning. After feeding Luca, Clove worked on her hair. Sandra gave her a light make-up. The beautician had been the previous day to give Amanda a manicure and wax her legs. Clove had cut her hair, as he did every Monday afternoon, along with the children's, Joan's, Stan's, Bob's, and Mark's when he arrived home.

Luca, Santorini, Lorenzo, Gessi (their and Amanda's Italian solicitor), their analyst, Sergio, and his financial advisor, analyst and PA flew from Italy to London in one of Luca's planes. On the Thursday evening they stayed in a hotel for the night, then travelled by express train to Chesterton, arriving early on Friday morning, where Lord Richard and Jack (Amanda's British solicitor) met them. When they arrived she recognised the quality of their suits. Luca and his sons were devastatingly handsome.

Amanda thought, 'Luca will look like these when he is grown-up – a heartbreaker.' She laughed to herself. Luca also resembled her brother Joshua, who was six foot three inches, had black curly hair and gorgeous features, and was full of charisma and fun.

Count Luca, with Lorenzo's, Santorini's and Amanda's permission, began with, "The four of us would like to buy your airline business, Sergio, but we couldn't take on your shipping business."

"That is fine with me, Luca. You are all very wise," he assured them, "I am very happy to let you have the business, which includes fourteen aeroplanes. You will have enough on with this with your reputation for safety. This takes commitment. The ships are getting old and worn out – a bit like me." He laughed. "I have had an offer for them. I will go ahead now that I know your requirements."

Luca then asked him, "Do you think they will buy our ships?"

"Very possibly yes, they will. I did mention this after our talk. May I ring, Lady Amanda?"

"Yes, please do, Signor Rossi."

He spoke in rapid Italian. He put his mobile away. "They are interested and await your contacting them," he said.

They all thanked him.

During coffee they discussed every detail. Sergio's analyst passed round reports of every aeroplane. They had to satisfy Lord Richard, Jack and Amanda before Lord Richard gave his approval to release the money to make Amanda a 40% shareholder. Luca, Lorenzo and Santorini invested 20% each. Amanda was thankful to have Richard and Jack on her side.

Luca, Lorenzo and Santorini expressed their gratitude for her investing her money. This was a new beginning for all of them and they were committed to ensuring that the planes were kept in good condition and their reputation for safety was maintained. The contracts would be finalised later that evening.

"The Contessa would be pleased I have used some of her legacy

16

in this way. This is what she would have done," Amanda assured the others.

They agreed.

Whilst Amanda went to feed Luca before lunch, they had a glass of champagne then freshened up and had a stroll with Stan, Bob and Joan. Sergio, Santorini and Lorenzo loved Chiverton and the setting. Jack and Richard stayed behind, discussing the business.

The Italians were thrilled with the children when they arrived home from school. They laughed when they saw how Sophie had grown. She was a beauty with her black curls and big black eyes. Then there was Luca with his black curls and big eyes. Mark was able to join them. The children lunched with Joan, Stan and Bob whilst the adults discussed the business and answered Mark's questions.

After a delicious relaxed lunch, they all complimented Amanda on the quality of the food and the wines. The wines! Amanda told them her father chose them and had them sent up. Then Mark had to leave them, and the children came back to say goodbye. Italian coffee was served outside at the table so the men could smoke their cigars. Then they met up again for an hour to conclude the business.

Amanda told Santorini and Lorenzo how devastating they looked, as always. She asked, "What material are your suits made from?"

They both told her it was a new fabric which was cooler to wear than other cloth.

Santorini asked, "Do you want some for your husband?"

"Yes please. Will you ask your tailor to send me samples? My beloved husband deserves the very best."

They both said, "Lucky Mark!"

Lorenzo promised to arrange for the samples to be sent.

Santorini told her, "You look gorgeous, darling. You always have done, but there is a new glow about you now." Looking at her breasts, he added, "Motherhood suits you."

She blushed. She was ready again to give Luca his feed.

Lorenzo asked, "Are you coming to Italy soon, darling?"

"Yes, we are."

"Good."

"Please be assured that you and your families will always be welcome here. You are a precious part of our family."

They thanked her.

"Dad loves to come," Lorenzo said.

"We love to have him."

They gave her hair, face, hand and body beauty products as well as a bottle of a new lightly fragranced perfume.

She was delighted.

She was eager to tell Mark about the new suit material, but she waited until they were soaking in their big bath before she told him what she had arranged. "Is this OK?" she asked.

"It is more than OK, my precious. Thank you."

He massaged her damaged leg, as always, then helped her out and they stood underneath the shower. He washed her hair and they dried themselves and put their robes on before Brenda brought baby Luca for his feed.

As they were drying, Mark thought (as he had many hundreds of times), 'How could she have wanted to marry me? She could have had her pick.' He once more thanked God.

"Of course, my precious darling, I want to look my best for you always," he said. He knew she liked him to wear well-fitted clothes.

"I'll ring Mr Schofield tomorrow to prepare him," Amanda promised.

"Lorenzo and Santorini are very smart, aren't they, sweetheart?"

"Yes, they always have been. Although they are Luca's sons, I know at times they have disappointed him."

"This is why he appreciates you, Amanda darling, our children and your parents, isn't it? He feels secure with us."

"He is selling his home and buying an apartment – also one in London near my parents. I am so pleased. I pray he will meet a suitable lady – he is so handsome and debonair, isn't he?"

Mark laughed. "Well, after marrying three times, perhaps he has had enough!"

"Very probably! He appears to be settled, and now he's happy about this new merger."

"I am so proud of you, my dearest wife."

"That's all I need, darling. Come on – it's been a long day. It's nearly time for our Luca."

"Did I tell you how utterly gorgeous you looked today."

"No, but I saw your face."

After Luca had been attended to and they were in bed, Mark told her how much he adored her and how thankful he was that she had married him. He cuddled her; then they fell asleep together.

The next day he told his colleagues Amanda was having a new suit made for him; her Italian friends had a new material, which was cooler to wear. They teased him and he replied, "I want my wife to be proud of me."

They understood. They all knew how Amanda liked well-fitted clothes. She had their greatest admiration for how she coped with her damaged knee, and they were very proud that she had married Mark and settled in the community. She treated everyone with respect.

News of the new airline merger spread on the grapevine, and the owner of a local factory, which made components for cars and aeroplanes, contacted Amanda to ask if there was any possibility of them helping. She acknowledged the request and promised to discuss it with her Italian partners.

Lorenzo had designed their aeroplanes. He had a masters degree in aeroplane design and engineering. He and Santorini, who also had a masters degree in engineering, made the parts and replacements for their aeroplanes. Their reputation for safety and personal commitment was well known. They knew they wouldn't be able to personally make all the parts for this new business, but they were determined to continue to supervise everything. Luca, Lorenzo and Santorini arranged to visit the Bryden factory with their analyst before committing themselves.

There was an excited buzz in the community. Men and women who had been made redundant through lack of orders looked forward to returning to their jobs.

The four men came to Chiverton for breakfast before spending the day at Searstons; the Messrs Searston had booked lunch at a first-class hotel. They returned to the factory. After discussion, Lorenzo told them the quality of their materials and workmanship was first class, but regretfully they wouldn't be able to cope with their demands.

Mr Searston senior told them truthfully, "With the recession, business has fallen off; most of our machines need replacing or upgrading. We have lost orders through not being able to meet the demands. I would like to retire, being now seventy-three years old, but I don't want to leave the burden with Simon."

Lorenzo knew their car-making unit was closed.

Mr Searston then said, "I will talk with Simon about selling up to give others an opportunity of buying to fulfil your requirements."

Simon came in with, "We need to do this, Dad; you have worked hard all your life. There is no way we can bring this factory up to date with the latest technologies."

Lorenzo promised to give them some work to do in the meantime.

Before setting off back to Italy, Luca rang Amanda. "We are satisfied with the workmanship and the materials used," he said, "but we regret, Amanda, that they cannot possibly fulfil all our requirements. They are talking of putting the factory up for sale to enable a business to buy who would install new machines and update the worn-out machines. Lorenzo is giving them some work in the meantime."

Over dinner, Amanda shared this news. The others knew orders had dropped off and redundancies had had to be made.

Whilst soaking in the bath, as Mark was massaging her leg, she suggested, "Perhaps I could help the community. What would you say to my asking Josh if he is willing to buy it with me? It is a wonderful opportunity, especially now that I am involved with the new airline merger."

Mark laughed. "Go for it, precious! You are a business lady. Your aunt would be proud."

"Thank you, darling. It is what she would do. She rescued businesses and had them built up. We need to get Josh up to discuss this."

She texted Joshua at home the next morning to tell him that she had a business proposition to discuss with him and Nicola.

He texted back later: 'I will come up Saturday morning. I had a non-urgent appointment but have rearranged this. As you know, Nicola takes Rose to ballet lessons, but we will ask the au pair if she is able to fill in. May I bring the other children?'

Amanda rang him that evening and told him she welcomed this.

"Nicola and I will bring the children on the early express train," Joshua replied. They liked this relaxed way of travelling and now the journey took under two hours.

Amanda rang Jack; he came to see her. She asked him to secretly enquire how much the factory would sell at; he set the wheels in motion and on the Friday rang her with an approximate figure. When he told her the price of buying and installing the six new machines they needed, she knew she couldn't afford that amount as well as the cost of restoring the old machines. Jack said he would come to see her the next morning. Lord Richard was coming too. Mark had to go to work.

Joshua admitted, "With my four children being educated, the running of our home and our Devon holiday home, I am willing to release money from investments but I haven't enough available to cover this amount."

Amanda admitted, "Neither have I, with buying into Signor Rossi's airline business, but, like Josh, I am interested. The question is, what can we do about it?"

Richard told them, "It is a marvellous investment opportunity. I wish I could afford it."

They all agreed to meet again.

When they were on their own, Amanda suggested to Joshua and Nicola that they ask their parents to release the trust fund they had for them.

"That's a good idea, Amanda, but I suspect it will still not be enough. Shall I ask them when we get back home?"

"Yes please, Josh."

When they were soaking in their bath before bed, Amanda told Mark about the meeting and said that she and Joshua hadn't enough capital.

Mark suggested, "What about selling the Villa Verona, sweetheart?"

Amanda froze. "How can you so much as suggest that, Mark? My aunt's beautiful home – all the memories I have! What about Sophie and Luca? They have Italian genes. Also, we make a good profit from letting it out; people appreciate being able to stay there for the operas." She stood up.

"Darling, I haven't massaged your leg," Mark said. He knew he had blown it.

He helped her out. She put a towel around herself, walked to the shower unit and tried to close the door. She and Mark always showered together.

"I can manage, thank you," she said.

He stood helpless and waited with his robe on to help her out. She resisted at first. "I am not entirely a cripple," she told him.

He dried her hair whilst she dried herself. He helped her put on her robe. She sat and applied moisturiser and hand cream. Whilst she was doing this he had a quick shower.

She was sat in her feeding chair in front of the window brushing her hair. Mark knew she was emotional just now. Her hormones were readjusting and she was coming to terms with the idea that Luca would be her last baby. They had decided six was enough as they wanted to be able to give them all the individual attention they needed. He firmly took the brush from her hand and began brushing as he always did. They were both silent. Mark was heartbroken, knowing he had hurt her. He thought of all she had done for him and his family. He paused in his brushing.

"Sweetheart, this is killing me. I am so sorry; I spoke without thinking. Please forgive me, darling."

"I am stupid, Mark, but please never say that again. It is a growing concern with the holiday guests paying."

He knelt at her side, cuddling her.

"I will never forget Andrew, and I will never forget Aunt Sophie, but if I hadn't you, even with our children, I wouldn't want to live," she said.

He couldn't believe what she had said; he knew she loved him but she was always emotional on the anniversary of her former fiancé's birthday and the date he was killed. Also as the children were growing up she never stopped regretting that her Aunt Sophie wasn't there to see them. Even after eight years she still missed her.

"Thank you for telling me, my precious wife. You could have married anyone."

Brenda knocked on the door; Mark fetched Luca for his feed and thanked her. He kissed and cuddled Luca. He passed him to Amanda. She cuddled and kissed him.

"Your daddy and I have had a misunderstanding," she said.

All Luca was interested in was his feed.

Amanda looked up at Mark with all the love she had for him in her eyes. He knelt down again and cuddled her and Luca. Luca stopped suckling and chuckled at them.

Mark exclaimed, "I think he understands."

Amanda laughed. "I wouldn't be surprised."

When Joan came to say goodnight and brought them their flask of hot, milky barley cup as always, Amanda told her, "Mark and I have had our first tiff."

"Oh well," she cheerfully said, "I have been told that making-up is very special."

After Brenda fetched Luca, it was.

Before drifting off sleep Mark thanked God for clearing away his insecurities about not being worthy of Amanda. He decided to encourage her to go ahead with Joshua in buying the factory.

He knew Amanda had discomfort at times in her leg, but she never complained. He had asked Sir Philip if there was anything further they could do to get the 100% bend, or ease the discomfort.

"Regretfully, no there isn't," was his reply. "The damage was so severe, affecting the ligaments and muscles, as you are aware, Chief Superintendent. This plastic knee is the very best there is. Unless infection sets in, leave well alone. You all know the signs to look for."

Mark asked, "If it became infected, what then?"

"That would be a serious concern; please do not think about that. Lady Amanda knows the score, and we all admire her greatly. If she continues with the swimming and exercises, her healthy diet and plenty of rest, everything should be fine. She is realistic enough to use her wheelchair when she needs to. If only there was a magic cure!" He shrugged his shoulders. "We will continue praying."

Mark replied, "Yes, that is the only way."

Amanda awoke at 4.50 a.m. Luca had slept through the night! She gently eased out of bed and had a quick wash with the door open. She sat in her robe brushing her hair, then changed into a flowered nursing nightdress and sprayed a dash of perfume. Mark slept on. She opened the bedroom door slightly for Brenda. After a few minutes, Brenda, beaming, brought Luca in. He had slept since his 10 p.m. feed. He hadn't even turned.

Amanda had every confidence in Brenda. She had been with them since the twins' birth. She knew Brenda kept a constant watch over the children during the night.

Amanda thanked her and said, "There must be something in the air: Chief Superintendent Mark is also still asleep."

Mark woke to hear Luca suckling and Amanda softly singing. He leapt out of bed and cuddled both of them.

Amanda told him, "Luca is a clever little chap. He slept all night."

Mark kissed and thanked him; then he went for his shower and shave.

He came out in his robe. Mrs Burton had brought their coffee and fruit juice. Brenda fetched Luca before Sally took over for the day.

"Sweetheart, I was thinking before going to sleep that you should go ahead with Josh and invest in the factory. This is really a wonderful opportunity. You obviously have inherited your aunt's business acumen."

"Thank you, darling. We need to get more information before committing."

She had been pondering over Mark's suggestion to sell the Villa Verona; she could buy a smaller one. The suites she, Mark and their family used were off-limits (as was the lake) to the guests who rented the Villa Verona all year round. Her aunt would have approved of her buying the factory; she had often rescued failing businesses in the same way. However, Amanda was filled with dread at the thought of losing this precious home. She prayed.

Mark silently regretted that he hadn't a vast amount of money to give her. He never squandered money, and he had invested ever since he began to earn, but he had always supported needy charities, especially the RSPCA and dogs' homes. Telling only his parents, he had paid Adam's university fees. He had been so glad Adam was adding to his school qualifications and following him to Cambridge. Mark had gained degrees there in music and languages, as well as learning a good deal that augmented his army leadership skills. Mark and his father had also encouraged Luke to go to university, but he had chosen not to go. Instead, he joined the police force, where he trained to be a fitness instructor, which was something he had wanted to do ever since he was a small boy.

Mark had suggested to Amanda that, with his share from the sale of his parents' home, they could install an outdoor pool with ten changing rooms complete with showers, toilets and central heating. After careful planning these were brick-built to the highest quality, in keeping with Chiverton, with de luxe fittings. These were a great blessing for visitors and resident swimmers.

"Precious, I will release my money from my mother to help you."

"Thank you, sweetheart, but please let that stay for our children's future with their grandmama giving this."

The very next morning, on Mark's desk was a letter from Chief Constable Blake notifying him of an appointment with him and the Divisional Commander for 9 a.m. in two days. After the appointment, he could have the remainder of the day off.

Mark texted Amanda and she texted back, teasing, 'If you are getting the sack, you will be able to run the factory for us.'

He worked through his lunchtimes, rearranging his schedules for the day off. Naturally he was wondering what the meeting was for. Was he going to be transferred? He kept this to himself. Amanda also was wondering this.

He immersed himself at work, and at home his family all lovingly supported him. When they were by themselves, he and Amanda talked about it.

The factory project was in abeyance whilst enquiries were being made. Lord Jonathan as a judge and Joshua in his capacity as a lawyer made enquiries; everything was above board. Searstons had the highest reputation, but Mr Searston senior was past retirement age and, as they already knew, the factory had lost orders because of having outdated machinery and because of the recession. Joshua shared this information with Amanda, who also had Lord Richard and Jack looking into all aspects of the company. Lord Richard informed Messrs Searston that he had a couple interested in buying their factory; that was all he could say at the moment.

Joshua promised to meet up with his parents to tell them about the factory. He went to see them and put them in the picture.

"With Amanda's approval I want to ask if the trust fund you set up for us both when we were born could be released to us. With Amanda buying into the larger airline business, she hasn't enough to cover this; neither have I. Although Nicola earns from her fashion magazine with Chelsea, I dare not release all my money. Our four children are coming up for university, and I also have the costs of running our home. Nicola has given me permission to borrow, and I am wondering whether to sell Seaways. Amanda is even considering selling the Villa Verona."

Teresa and Jonathan looked horrified.

"Darling Josh," his mother broke in, "you and Amanda do not have to concern yourselves. The trust fund your dad and I set up for you both when you were born hasn't been touched. We offered this to Amanda and you when she was moving into Chiverton, and you both assured us you were OK. You wanted the fund to continue making a good profit. Also, darling, your dad knows and will approve." (He nodded.) "We have money invested for you both for when we die. This can also be released. I am so thankful you have been able to talk to us about this."

"Gosh, thanks, Mum, Dad." He kissed them both.

Jonathan told him, "Your mum and I are very proud of you and Amanda. We always have been. You are a wonderful son and daughter, and we admire the way you always worked hard at school and university, and in your careers. We were doubtful when you first brought Nicola home to meet us – a glamorous model that looked as though she never ate. I confess at the time I thought, 'Oh dear!' How wrong I was! We couldn't wish for a more loving daughter-in-law and mother to our grandchildren, and we are very grateful to her for making you happy. If Richard approves the Derbyshire factory as a good investment, we are only too happy to release the money. It is yours and Amanda's."

"Thanks, Dad. I know you will not disclose to Amanda what I have told you about the Villa Verona. I am confident she will tell you herself. I know I haven't told you both – and I am not saying this because of the money," he laughed – "but you have been wonderful parents to us. You have always set us a good example; you have never squandered money. This is why I am being careful to make sure I set my children that same example. As you both know, living in London is expensive."

Amanda, of course, told her mother about the local factory, and Teresa then repeated to her the details of the investments she had. "We'll leave the trust funds unless or until you and Josh need them," she said.

"Oh, Mum, you and Dada are the tops! With expert management it could run as smoothly as Mason's. Our aunts would be so pleased that Josh and I are using their inheritance in this way."

Jonathan and Joshua came to meet Amanda on the very early train in order to greet Mark and the children before they left. They breakfasted whilst travelling; they both laughed when they realised this was the first time in years they had spent a morning together. They had to get back early for appointments.

When Jonathan told them the amount they had released for them both, Joshua exclaimed, "We don't need as much as that, Dad!"

Amanda verified this.

"Your mum and I know, but please accept it. It's such a pleasure to help you both and your families. Gray has organised these investments to continue, so we haven't lost out too much."

Joshua then suggested to Amanda, "We could reopen the car-making unit again."

"Yes, good idea! We need to look fully into this."

Jonathan was again reminded how efficient they were – how they thought laterally and not impulsively. They had a prayer time and praised God together. Then Stan came to take them back to the station.

Amanda went to feed Luca. She sat cuddling him in front of her bedroom window, looking out at the glorious scenery and giving God her personal thanks.

Then Crystal fetched Luca, and Amanda went to play her piano before Sarah and Angela came to walk with her and Luca.

Reflecting on what Joshua had told him and Teresa about being wonderful parents, Jonathan began to think about Teresa in a new way. He adored her and appreciated all she had done for him: supporting him in his career, entertaining his colleagues, putting him first, and always looking immaculate for him. She was the most unselfish lady there could be. He decided to do something very special to show his appreciation.

At the time he was appearing as judge in an important court case, but when that was over he arranged to have a week off and asked Teresa to keep this time free. She usually went to Mason's for a few hours on most weekdays, but she did as Jonathan requested.

He told her he was taking her away from Monday to Friday.

She enquired, "Where are we going, darling?"

"It's a surprise, sweetheart."

"How will I know what to pack? We may be going to Iceland!"

He laughed. "No, Teresa, it isn't there. What about Paris?"

"Paris! I am thrilled, my precious husband. Have I forgotten some anniversary?"

"No, you have not, but I have realised that I have always taken you for granted. After what Josh said to us, this is going to change."

"I couldn't be happier than I am and have been, beloved. I thank God every day you married me."

They kissed passionately.

"See," she teased, "we do not have to go to Paris!"

He laughed. "Would you like to travel on the Eurostar train?"

"Yes, it will be most interesting, thank you, sweetheart."

When they told Amanda and Joshua, they were over the moon.

Chapter 3

Amanda encouraged Mark to wear one of his new suits with a white shirt and new tie for his meeting with the Chief Constable. He queried this.

"Is it a bit over the top, darling?"

"No," she firmly said, "you are my husband and a wonderful police officer."

The children hadn't been told of the meeting, and breakfast was as normal apart from the fact that Mark didn't eat with his usual hearty appetite. Amanda had a space with him before his assistant picked him up.

The Chief Constable's PA took Mark into the office. Also there was the Deputy Chief Constable with the Divisional Commander. They all smilingly greeted Mark.

The Chief Constable asked him to sit down and began: "I have some sad news to tell you, Mark. My wife is in the early stage of dementia."

Mark was shocked and expressed his sympathy.

"As you know, we have a daughter, Mildred." (She was a head teacher in Plymouth, unmarried.) "I am retiring and selling up here to buy a home near Mildred. She asked us to live with her, but she has her own life and career. There are first-class care supports here, but for my wife's dignity, and to make it easier for Mildred, I have decided to move. Now I have put you in the picture."

Mark shook his head; he was stunned by this news.

"For the last few weeks we have been observing you, Mark, and we all, of one accord, are asking you to take over from me. You have the qualities, expertise and training for this position."

He paused again. Mark was swallowing. "You have the greatest respect from everyone."

"I thought I was being transferred," Mark told everyone.

They laughed. "Oh, no, no!"

Mark was filled with thankfulness that he wasn't being transferred, and for the honour of this promotion.

"Please talk it over with Lady Amanda. We are aware you have six young children to spend time with, and of course your wife, so be assured we would not throw you in at the deep end, as they say. You will be well supported. We have every confidence in you, Mark."

"Thank you, sir. I am very honoured. This is such a shock to me. I am deeply sorry about your wife."

"Thank you, Mark. As you know, she is very dignified, and we wish to maintain a low profile. She has always supported me, ever since we married, and I am going to ensure she has a good quality of life in the time she has left. Would you like a coffee, Mark?"

"Yes please, sir."

Whilst they were waiting for the coffee, the Chief Constable said to Mark, "We know Lady Amanda has always supported you in your work and will continue to do so. We want you to know, Mark, that it is because we believe in your merit that we offer you this promotion."

"Thank you, sir."

They all discussed what the job would entail. Then they stood up and shook Mark's hand.

Chief Constable Blake told him, "We know this must be a shock, so how would you like to go home for the day to talk it over with your wife?"

"Thank you, sir. I appreciate this."

He was taken home, and en route he texted Amanda: 'I am on my way home, darling. I haven't been sacked or transferred.'

She and Luca were waiting outside for him. After kissing and cuddling them he ran upstairs and changed his clothes. Then they went walking and he told her what had transpired.

She also was deeply shocked about Mrs Blake. "I am very proud of you, Mark. I was before this. You have all the qualities necessary to succeed in this most important role. I will support you, darling. We will now forget about the factory."

"Please don't, Amanda; this will be even more important now."

"Right," she said, "we will continue keeping it secret, darling. This is your time now – I insist. It's what you have earned. You have always worked hard in the army and the police. You will be a wonderful Chief Constable. You are senior to me now," she teased. "I will have to watch it. Come on, sweet – the children have come home for lunch."

The children ran up to them shouting, "Daddy! Daddy!"

"Would you like me to take you back to school? I have the afternoon off."

"Yes please. Will you be able to fetch us home, Daddy?"

"Yes, I will; and then what shall we do?"

"Fly our kites," they all shouted.

Mark admired them. Even though he had the afternoon off, they accepted they had to go back to school. He gathered them all up, cuddling them.

Amanda took the children upstairs to freshen up. They quickly came back down. Stan, Bob and Joan were beaming. They had tears in their eyes. They dare not say anything in front of the children, because it would be passed on to their teachers!

The children did tell their teachers that their father had the afternoon off and was fetching them home; then they were going to fly their kites! All the children from the classes wanted to go and fly kites with them.

When Mark returned to the school at home time, Mrs Vine's PA was waiting for him. She asked if he could spare Mrs Vine a few minutes whilst he was waiting for Holly and Vincent. She would bring the triplets in to him as they were excited he was able to fetch them home.

Mrs Vine offered him coffee, and she had fruit drinks prepared for the triplets. She told him about the class wanting to fly kites.

Mark promised her, "I will mention this to Lady Amanda."

"I need your permission for Vincent and Holly to have an IQ test, sir. They are so intelligent and we all know they are capable of doing the work in a more advanced class. They are mature enough to fit in with the older children. As you know, we encourage them to mix together."

"Thank you, Mrs Vine. This is wonderful news. My wife will agree to this, I know. I will talk to her about it. A similar thing happened to her when she was at school."

Mrs Vine went on: "The triplets also are a delight. Eric is highly intelligent and like Vincent and Holly his concentration and memory recall are first class. Heather also is intelligent and applies herself, but at times she goes into a 'dream time'. We realise this is owing to her creative side. Sophie also is intelligent. Sophie is Sophie – full of drama!"

They both laughed.

"We are so grateful to you all. The children eagerly come to school each morning," Mark sincerely told her.

The triplets were brought in; they spontaneously ran up to Mark, kissed him and stood with their arms around him.

"If only all children were so loved and secure, Chief Superintendent." Mrs Vine sighed.

"We are so God-blessed to have them."

"We admire how you are bringing them up to enjoy simple pleasures."

"Thank you, Mrs Vine."

Whilst the children were having their drinks, the PA brought Vincent and Holly. They too kissed and cuddled their father.

Mrs Vine asked about Luca, and then said, "I had better let you go for the kite-flying."

She shook hands with Mark, and he and the triplets thanked her for the drinks.

Later, when Mark related what Mrs Vine had said, Amanda immediately suggested that they could perhaps have a Sunday afternoon kite-flying with the parents and children. She also was thrilled about the IQ test. She had coped at school and she knew they would. Holly, Vincent and the triplets were at the private school, but they always mixed in the community at the police Saturday afternoons, the local spring fairs and other happenings, such as the Chatsworth House shows.

With Vincent, Amanda sent a note to the headmistress asking if she thought a Sunday afternoon would be a good idea for the kite-flying, and, if so, would the teachers and families care to join in? Then everyone could come back for afternoon tea. She suggested that coming Sunday at 2.30 p.m. The forecast was for fine and breezy weather.

Mrs Vine and Miss Bracken thought this was wonderful. They filled in the day and time and gave out the invitations Amanda had sent.

When Amanda and Mark were soaking in the bath that evening, Mark thoughtfully reflected, "Amanda, sweetheart, haven't we wonderful children? They didn't ask for the afternoon off school; they chose to fly their kites and play in the wood when they could have asked for so much more."

They both went quiet.

Amanda invited the Duke and Duchess, and Richard and Sarah, to the afternoon. The invitations were received with delight. They all accepted with joy.

Thankfully it was a windy afternoon, as the forecast had predicted, and it was a great success. Luca's pram had a kite-shaped balloon attached! Richard, Sarah and Angela came with the Duke and Duchess. Amanda was in her battery-powered wheelchair.

It was such a happy time – a real eye-opener. The men, including the Duke, ran about enjoying themselves. Most of the children had never seen their fathers, who were all busy businessmen, playing in this way before; in fact, some of them had been so busy that they had forgotten what it was like to have fun. It was a new beginning.

Afterwards Mark congratulated Amanda and told her it was another step in getting to know the community, parents and teachers through relaxing, healthy fun.

"It's a great blessing having the field fenced off to keep the animals out, sweetheart. I think it wouldn't have been appreciated if anyone had slipped into a cowpat or other droppings." He laughed.

Amanda laughingly agreed.

Over the years when more calves and lambs were born, Mr Shulot's eldest son, Guy, worked full-time instead of part-time to attend to these and the chickens. Six years before, Guy had suggested that Amanda buy some goats, which she did. Guy and his dad, milked the cows and goats. They all loved the goats' milk, and Gerald made yoghurts. A cheese factory bought the surplus milk. Stan and Bob made soaps.

Guy obligingly collected the sheep droppings and made these into a liquid fertiliser for the greenhouses and gardens. The manures were put on the 'special' compost heap. Amanda and Mark let him keep his horses in a fenced-off field so they didn't run and knock her over. Amanda always made time whenever Guy or Mr Shulot had anything to ask or discuss, and she regularly talked to them.

Tarquin had been too strong for Amanda. She could no longer ride him or any other horse, but he kept, in his loving way, knocking her over. She tried breaking her fall using the tuck-and-roll move she had learnt with the SAS, but with her damaged knee this didn't work. He had a 100% pedigree bloodline, so he went to a known and trusted stud farm, where he lived with the herd and got to know the mares before he performed. He was very happy. Amanda kept up to date with his progress; she greatly missed him. It was frustrating not being able to ride, and it had been a hard decision to have him transferred to the stud farm. It was very costly having him cared for, but the sale of the foals more than compensated. She kept a diary of the horses he had mated with, the names of his offspring and their progress. She, the children and whoever was around watched the television coverage of the horse racing at the York Ebor Festival. They had all been to this and the local St Leger two years ago, and they promised to return when Luca was older. Amanda always recorded these and the Derby, Goodwood, the Oaks and Royal Ascot. She also recorded whenever Tarquin's foals were racing. She still felt pangs of regret at being unable to ride, but she was happy to watch or read anything related to horses.

Vincent brought a letter home from Mrs Vine: 'We thank you for the kite-flying afternoon. We all enjoyed it. We are all hoping for a repeat at some stage! The children are drawing and designing kites in their arts-and-crafts lessons.'

Chapter 4

Amanda invited her parents, Joshua, Nicola and their family up for Saturday lunch. She asked them to make a special effort to come as she and Mark had some exciting news to share.

Joshua joked to Nicola, "Is she expecting again?"

They all travelled up on the express train – they enjoyed these journeys. Rose forfeited her ballet for the day. Luke and Stan met them at the station.

Amanda, Joan, Mark, Adam, Uncle Bob and the children were outside waiting to greet them. After coffee and fresh fruit drinks for the children, they and Rose ran off to see the ponies. Julian and Sandra brought champagne. The staff knew there was something exciting happening; Amanda had requested Sandra to come in on her day off.

Mark waited until everyone had been served and Julian and Sandra had left them. He stood up, cleared his throat and announced, "I am being promoted to Chief Constable of this area."

They all jumped up and hugged him. Amanda was crying with pride. They congratulated him and echoed the opinion that he was the perfect man for the job.

When they had celebrated, they went to join the children, and after sharing lunch the family returned to London.

Amanda had arranged for Mrs Burton, Gerald, Sandra and Julian to join them after lunch, bringing two bottles of champagne and glasses. When Mark and Luke had served them, he told them of his promotion. They were very pleased and excited at this. They congratulated him.

Adam went to do some illustrating, and Mark and Amanda took the children swimming. Luke, having had the morning off, went into his fitness studio. Everyone was so happy at Mark being honoured in this way.

Chief Constable Blake gave the local networks and the reporters the news that he was taking early retirement and going to live near his daughter in Plymouth. He declared, "I and my colleagues are very proud to announce that Chief Superintendent Mark Young is being promoted to take my place as Chief Constable from the beginning of June."

Everyone cheered and clapped.

An interview with the local media was arranged for the promotion morning and Mark agreed to be filmed informally afterwards at Chiverton.

When the coverage of the promotion morning was shown, they included Mark's achievements at school and at university, during his army career and since joining the police. His ex-tutors offered their congratulations and said that Mark had always worked hard and had a razor-sharp brain. His army superior gave him the highest praise, and he also mentioned Mark's razor-sharp brain and how he gave 100% of himself. The Divisional Commander gave a glowing report of Mark's achievements since joining the force. He described the way the men respected Mark and listened to him, and said he was full of integrity and truth. Whenever Mark had to rebuke someone he did it privately, and this added to the respect everyone had for him.

The local networks and reporters came to Chiverton and Mark, dressed casually, gave them an informal interview. He sat on the settee in the sitting room cuddling Luca; some of the dogs were round his feet.

Amanda thought, 'He looks very dishy.'

She, the children and the other dogs were stood out of camera range.

He answered their questions and told them, "I am looking forward to this challenge. My wife and I are deeply sorry about Mrs Blake's illness, and the family are in our prayers. I believe I will do a better job because of my good fortune in having my wife and children. If I was still single, I wouldn't understand what being a husband and father entails. I have contact with and understanding of school life and I am aware of children's needs. I am very blessed in having had the opportunity to get to know local families as well as my police colleagues. Family life is very important to me and I will be encouraging families to share their experiences together."

He answered more questions and told them, "Yes, we are having a celebration lunch on Friday the 15th of May. We are having a week's holiday in Devon with my brother-in-law and family at the beginning of May. My wife and I regret that our children will be missing school, but as the school is closed for May Day they will only miss four days. We have Mrs Vine's permission, and they will continue their homework. It's sensible for us to have this break before I begin my new job."

They thanked him and wished him all the best.

Smiling, he disconnected his microphone and beckoned his family over. He stood up and helped Amanda to sit. He put his arm round her waist; she put her arm round his shoulder and the other on Luca. The children then sat down so that they were all close together and they smiled at the cameras. The crew were all delighted at this informal interview and the pictures.

Cards and letters of congratulation and best wishes poured in for Mark.

Amanda, in a discussion with Stan, Mark and Luke, told them, "Josh and I would like to give Adam the opportunity of taking on the job as business manager of the factory; with his degrees he has all the qualifications needed."

They gave their full approval, but of course it was up to Adam.

Amanda had a talk with Adam. She asked him several questions and was satisfied with his answers. He was thrilled at being asked to join into this factory and use his skills. She then asked him if he agreed to meet with his father and brothers and put them in the picture. He, of course, welcomed this.

They set up an informal meeting and Amanda told them, "Adam is joining the factory as business manager. He is young, but Josh and I know he will make a good job of it. I was wondering a few days ago if it would be too much for him just now, and I remembered when I first came to Ashwood to recuperate and I hosted for the very first time Mark's promotion lunch. I was nervous, but with help it was a success."

They all agreed.

"It was a new beginning for me, and I can safely say that I soon organised lunches with confidence. This is how I see Adam: with help he will do his best, and then he too will grow in confidence. Adam knows that although he is my beloved brother-in-law, I and Joshua will treat him as an employee. Therefore he will have to apply himself. He knows he can come to us with any problem he is doubtful about. Finally, I congratulate Adam in this new role and wish him every success."

They all clapped. Adam hugged her and laughed. "I should not do this, Amanda – only at home. I should treat you with the greatest respect and call you Lady Amanda or ma'am."

She laughed. She loved him dearly – as she did Luke – and everyone knew it.

After Stan's dog had died from old age, he bought a trained Dobermann from a reputable breeder. Mark bought a trained golden retriever puppy for the children from their vet after, heartbreakingly, he had to have his dog put down. Arthritis had set in where Monty had been ill treated before Mark had found him abandoned.

These were active walking dogs, just right as companions for Stan on his own, or with Bob and their friends, to take walking over the beautiful Derbyshire moors. They were also very good with children. Stan and Mark wouldn't have had them otherwise.

Mark and Amanda bought Stan a newly designed pocket-sized personal waterproof navigation system, battery operated for pocket or wrist, for his birthday. He was thrilled with all the different technologies it incorporated.

"Thank you very much, both of you. It will be very useful when I am on my own on the moors – especially if I feel ill or fall, or come across anyone in need of help. I will be able to ring and give my exact location from the tracking system. The same applies if any of my pals need help."

It was full of useful outdoor technology. They were all grateful for this. All the males at Chiverton and the twins and triplets, who loved indoor and outdoor games, put this personal navigator on their next requested-presents list.

Sparky was old now and not active. He had a basket in the playroom. They took him down to the river or into the wood in Heather's doll's pram. When it was raining or windy they put the hood up. When they got to the wood they put a blanket down for him to lie on and sniff the smells of the woodland.

One Saturday afternoon they knew he was at the end. Mark laid him gently on the blanket and stayed nearby whilst the children played. Then he knew Sparky had gone. He stood crying. They all rushed up to him and cried.

Luke covered Sparky, picked and him up and carried him to the house. He rang Miles, the vet. It was an answerphone, so he left a message. He went back to join the family. They were still stood discussing having a stone made, as they had for previous dogs. Amanda suggested they plant a tree also.

Amanda's Rottweiler, Thunder, and Cambridge and Oxford, the German shepherds who had been police sniffer dogs, were also getting old and not as mobile; they too had the greatest care and love.

One day as Amanda was strolling with Luca, Sarah and Angela, Mr Shulot asked if he might have a word with her. Amanda excused herself to Sarah.

"We have the pups due next week, ma'am – the ones that I mentioned to you; would you still like a couple of them?"

"Yes please, Mr Shulot."

She knew Mr Shulot's dogs had good bloodlines and she thought they would replace the ache in her heart when Thunder, Cambridge and Oxford died.

"Very good, ma'am. When you have chosen I will train them for you."

"Thank you, Mr Shulot."

Mark replaced Sparky with another highly recommended Jack Russell pup from their vet. Amanda called him Derby.

Sarah was laughing. "You love dogs, don't you, darling?"

"I do, Sarah – especially now that I cannot ride a horse."

When Amanda told Mark about the German shepherd pups being due next week, he teased her: "How many more?"

"When Thunder dies I would like a Dobermann. They are gorgeous."

"OK, darling."

The Shulot German shepherds were brilliant dogs. The children weren't afraid of them. Mr Shulot kept them fenced off during the day when they weren't out walking with him. At night they freely roamed the grounds. They never disturbed the Chiverton dogs. They kept Chiverton free of rats and mice. They also frightened the foxes off and kept the rabbits out of the vegetable gardens.

A meeting was set up at Chiverton for that Saturday morning, with Messrs Searston, their solicitor, production manager and foreman. Joshua brought his solicitor; Amanda, Lord Richard, Jack, the analyst they had brought in and Adam were also there.

Joshua and his solicitor travelled up on the express train with the twins (Andrew and David) and Susan. Nicola had taken Rose to her ballet class. Then they planned to lunch together and go to a ballet matinee.

The twins and triplets groomed their ponies and cleaned their tackle on Saturday mornings with the help of a reputable young man who was training to be a vet; he was glad of the money he earned from this job. Their cousins offered to help them. Stan and Joan were nearby.

Mark had to work, but he knew Amanda would fill him in later.

Lord Richard opened the casual meeting with the news: "Lady Amanda and Mr Dansie are buying the factory. Lady Amanda has asked for this news not to be broadcast as yet. As her husband has recently been promoted to Chief Constable, Amanda insists that this should be his time."

They all smiled at her.

Messrs Searston, the production manager (John), the foreman (Gavin) and Mr Weston (the analyst) had brought all the details. Gavin told them all the machines needed updating or replacing.

John informed them it was a sound business and would thrive again with new machines and the orders from Italy.

"Mr Adam Young is joining the company with his administration skills. He has a masters degree in business studies and economics from Cambridge University, but he and his family need to know, this being his first job, what the job of manager will entail," Richard asked them.

Mr Searston senior reassured them: "We will be happy to stay on part-time for a few weeks to advise him."

This was welcomed by everyone.

"Mr Young is welcome to come in now, but with respect to Lady Amanda – and, ma'am, we have the greatest respect and admiration for how you are supporting your husband – this would let the cat out of the bag, as they say."

They all laughed.

Simon Searston then told them, "We have John and Gavin – and, believe me, there are no better. They will help and advise when asked; the office staff are committed to their jobs, and they will also give their support. In fact, I am so excited at this new beginning that I am asking if you will take me on part-time as a member of your staff. My wife is already moaning about how I shall get under her feet."

They all laughed again.

Joshua came in with, "My sister and I will be grateful for any help, please. Lady Amanda is of course busy with Luca, who is only three months old, her other children and her husband. I am a busy lawyer in London, as you know. I also have a wife and four growing children."

Tony Searston reassured them: "Everyone will help to the best of their abilities. They will be so pleased the factory will remain open with the Italian aeroplane work, and also, when they know Lady Amanda and you, Mr Dansie, are buying, there will be great rejoicing and thankfulness."

Amanda and Joshua thanked him.

Simon asked, "May we promise the redundant staff that they will be reinstated?"

Joshua asked, "Can we leave this with you, Mr Searston?"

"We will also begin replacing the worn parts in the machines and order the six new machines. Speed is of the essence as we have deadlines to meet. The new technology will enable us to turn out parts quickly whilst still retaining the quality of work we have always taken pride in."

John, Gavin and Mr Weston endorsed that.

Lord Richard expressed the need for a further meeting. "Are Saturday mornings convenient? If we could meet here again, it would help Lady Amanda whilst she is feeding Luca."

They all laughed and said, "Yes, please."

Coffee was served.

Messrs Searston, John, Gavin and Mr Weston left and rushed back to the factory. They discussed Lady Amanda and how impressed they were with her efficient no-nonsense manner. She was a businesswoman. She would bring plenty of orders in.

Lord Richard and Jack went home. Joshua's solicitor went to catch his train back to London. Richard had two financial advisors working for him now, but he personally dealt with Chiverton and kept the records in secure files.

Amanda liked the Messrs Searston, John and Gavin, and she looked forward to getting to know them. She identified with their straight and respectful way of talking. She had quickly become accustomed to this eight years before, when she first came to Derbyshire. As she had relaxed she realised that her speech was too formal, so she had slightly adjusted.

Amanda and Joshua went to find the children, who were having the time of their lives! She then went upstairs to Luca, thanking God the way ahead for the factory looked smooth.

Local people noticed the Messrs Searston, John and Gavin going to Chiverton, and speculation grew that Lady Amanda was buying the factory. Everyone hoped so; they trusted her and they were hopeful that she would bring in aeroplane orders from Italy. It was passed on that the meetings were to discuss the Italian orders – which wasn't a lie.

Her publishers asked Amanda to write another children's story. Her last three were still selling, and they were very popular; they were read in schools and regularly borrowed from libraries. Children loved them. She began to write a humorous story about Sparky, and she again asked Adam and Heather to do some illustrations.

Amanda didn't go to church whilst she was feeding Luca. She hadn't been in her first and third trimester, as before. Stan, Luke, Adam, Joan and Bob went to The Open Church. Holly and Vincent went with them, and the first Sunday of each month they worshipped at the local churches family service in a rota. Mark and the triplets went with them to these.

All the children had Bible-reading notes, which they discussed with Mark and Amanda. Mark went to The Open Church when it was his turn to play the organ, but they understood when he stayed with Amanda at other times. Amanda didn't invite the ministers and their families to her home during this time, but the Reverend Matthew was always welcome.

After lunch, when Luca had been fed and attended to, they all went for a walk by the river. The dogs, as always, enjoyed themselves in the water. Afterwards the children went for a swim with Mark, Luke, Adam and Matthew. They were proficient swimmers now. Mark showered with his boys. Joan supervised the girls and the hair-washing. Then, after afternoon tea, Matthew went home and Amanda and Mark had their Sunday evening with all the children playing games and talking together before supper and bed.

Chapter 5

Adam asked to speak with his father, Mark, Luke and Amanda. They cleared a space.

"What shall I do about the unit? Mother gave me the money towards this."

"She will not mind how you use it, but have you thought about renting it out?" Mark asked him.

"It will be a good investment," his father suggested.

"I need advice on this," Adam declared. "Is it OK if I ask Lord Richard?"

"He will be pleased to help," Amanda assured him.

"I will ask him, then – professionally, of course."

They laughed.

"You sound like a business manager already," teased Luke.

Adam told Mr Lee that he had had another business opportunity and so he would be renting this unit out.

Mr Lee enquired, "How much are you asking? If the price is right, will you let me have it? My business is expanding so much that this unit would be very useful for me as well as the larger one."

Richard had advised him on what rent to ask.

Mr Lee, after thinking for a few minutes, agreed and they shook hands. Adam then told him he would have the papers drawn up.

Adam told his employers, Messrs Knutt at the Graphics Store, that he needed to leave in one month.

They looked disappointed but said, "We have been expecting you to set up on your own."

"No, I'm not doing that. I can't at the moment tell you what I will be doing."

Mr Knutt senior then asked, "Will you possibly be able to illustrate the cards for Ryman's? You brought that business in and we won't be able to cope with it without you."

"That's a thought, sir. I suppose I could illustrate on Saturdays."

"You would be most welcome to stay all day if that will suit you."

"Thank you. I should be able to do that."

"Another thought, Adam, is that they gave us the order on the understanding you would be illustrating. What about you taking this contract and doing the work from Chiverton? You would then know the deadlines you have to meet. You have helped us, Adam, and brought other ongoing work in. We can manage that. Think about it and let us know."

"Thank you, Mr Knutt. I will ask my family. And also, I thank you for all you have done for me. I have really enjoyed being here. Is it all right if I leave in one month, then?"

They agreed to this and shook hands.

Adam went to start work.

When Adam shared this with his family they were delighted that he wouldn't be giving up his art.

"You will have your own graphics business soon," Luke teased him.

"That's an idea, broth'. It's something for me to think about in the future. I could rent out illustrators' desks in the unit."

Stan asked, "What is that?"

Adam told him: "It is like the owner of a hairdressing salon renting off chairs to individual hairdressers. I need to find out more about this."

"Don't get swollen-headed," teased Luke.

"Miss Land may be able to help you," his father suggested slyly. They had been wondering what had happened to this budding romance.

"Oh no! She is the last person. She is too pushy – not suitable at all."

"Did she want you to marry her after the first date," Luke teased again.

"Something like that," Adam laughed. "I am OK with my pals – the females are good sports."

"You will have to watch out when you are manager of Dansie & Young," Amanda also teased him.

He laughed. He was used to being teased by them, and he was glad they had stopped treating him like their baby brother. He knew he could bring his friends to Chiverton any time. Amanda had always insisted it was his and Luke's home.

Ryman's welcomed him continuing to illustrate for them, and a contract was being drawn up. They told him the price for 100 assorted cards. Adam was astounded. They asked if he could also supply a verse and greetings for each card.

He asked Amanda and Mark if he might work from home on Saturdays producing these illustrations. They welcomed him using his talent and told him to choose a suitable room. All the rooms had good light. He settled on one at the back so that he wouldn't disturb the children.

He thought about the verses, and he decided to ask Robert, who had been a friend since before Amanda and Mark married. He wasn't just showing favouritism among his pals; Robert was good with words. Mark had paved the way for Robert to get a computer job in police finance eight years before, and he had gone from strength to strength, gaining everyone's respect. His father, the vicar of St James', had had his licence renewed for a further seven years.

Adam rang Robert and told him about the Saturday work. He asked, "What do you think about doing the verses and greetings for these cards? I can have a contract drawn up by Ryman's for you to do this work. The contract would be yours."

Robert couldn't believe it. "Thanks, Adam," he said. "You are a star. I will, please. As you know, I need a new car."

"Right, we'll talk on Sunday evening when I pick you up." (Adam and Robert went to The Open Church youth service. His other pals also went, but Adam told them he had something to discuss with Robert as they were travelling. They were able to get there in their cars.) Adam told Robert, "We'll need to start getting the equipment."

Robert suggested, "Online?"

"Yes, good idea! However, I thought we should support the community: there is a brilliant arts-and-crafts shop in Chesterton. We need to make a list and then Dad will drop it off. This will give them a chance to get everything together and perhaps order in anything they don't have in-store. Are you able to come to Chiverton next Saturday to make a start sorting out?"

"Yes please, Adam."

"I'll pick you up at 9 a.m. We may have to call in at Chesterton. Then for lunch I could ask Mrs Burton for some sandwiches, fruit and coffee. Then we can stretch our legs. The kids will expect us to go into the wood with them for the afternoon, as I have been doing a lot recently, but when they know we have to work they'll understand."

"That's brill with me, Adam."

"Unfortunately, we'll have to pay tax."

They both groaned.

They shared this news with their pals, who were pleased for them. They said that if there was anything they could do – any running about or whatever – they hoped Adam or Robert would let them know. The two men promised they would and thanked them. Adam dare not tell them about Dansie & Young yet.

When Adam explained to the children what he and Robert would be doing on Saturday afternoons, Heather asked, "May I draw some pictures, Uncle Adam, please?"

"Yes, darling, thank you."

Heather loved sketching; she had obviously inherited her artistic flair from her grandfather, Stan. Sophie also drew, but her interest was in fashion sketches!

Vincent then asked, "May I take photographs of flowers, trees and leaves in the wood?"

"Yes please."

That started it: all the children then wanted to take photographs.

Adam said, "We had better ask your parents' permission."

Amanda and Mark of course agreed.

Vincent had a good camera he had bought with his birthday money. His brother and sisters asked their Uncle Luke to help them choose, so, as he knew a lot about cameras, he took them to the shop and advised them which to buy.

Stan suggested, "Perhaps you can take ideas from my sketches, Adam?"

He thanked him. "Brill, Dad! As long as the cards are originals, all this will be fine."

Adam had a lovely warm feeling because he appreciated the way his family were supporting him. He thanked God for them.

Amanda was over the moon at Mark's promotion; he would no longer be in her shadow. Amanda had made it clear that he was the head of the household, but it was well known that the Contessa had bought Amanda their home and provided money.

She ordered five fitted shirts from Brookwell to match Mark's new suits. When these were ready she went to collect them and bought him new ties. She loved to pop into Brookwell.

Mark's colleagues often referred to when Lady Amanda was a commander at the Met, and how she dealt with the most hardened criminals without allowing it to affect her. Mark pointed out that she was highly trained and worked with the SAS; it also helped that her family supported her, her father being a High Court judge and her brother a highly respected lawyer.

"She also had good support from the Met – but, even so! She has my greatest respect and awe. To deal with all she had to, she must be made of good stuff. Also, thankfully, she has her faith in Jesus."

On their own the unbelievers discussed this:

"Jesus didn't stop her fiancé being killed, her knee shattered and her team being killed," one said.

"To be fair, such killings and injuries are part of a world created by man."

They all had to agree with that.

"When Mark takes over as Chief Constable, I will have to dress in keeping with his position, Mum, don't you agree? My casuals are OK, but when I start going to church again and out and about I will need to be a bit more sophisticated."

"You always look beautiful, darling, with your complexion and shining hair; you have regained your figure again. I will get the latest fashion designs and patterns from Nicola; then I will send for the materials."

"Thank you, Mum."

Teresa texted Nicola with her request and Nicola responded with pleasure.

Amanda told Jean her needs.

"I look forward to making these, ma'am."

"What would I do without you, Jean?"

"There are plenty of others who would like to be in my shoes," she replied. "May I ask Mrs Doyle to help me finish the settee and chair covers and cushions whilst you are away, now the decorators have finished? I will then be able to concentrate on your new clothes."

"Whatever you think, Jean! You know I trust and appreciate you. You are making a beautiful job, Jean, and the curtains look lovely."

"Thank you, ma'am. It is always a pleasure to make anything for you."

Teresa texted Amanda: 'I've received the patterns from Nicola; I will send these for your approval. I have e-mailed you pictures of some new beautiful pure silks covered with tiny multicoloured flowers. There is a black, darling. I can just see you in this. It's unique. I also have some pure wool challis coming in; it will make up into lovely two-piece suits for the autumn. There is a lilac/pink tweed, also gold/lemon and gorgeous different-coloured heathers. I can picture you in these. You have your mannequin for hats, darling. Is there anything else you need whilst the delivery van is coming up?"

Amanda rang and told her, "You are a star, Mum; I'll make a list to go on my account."

Chiverton got through towels and face cloths very quickly. She added bedding and pillows. She bought as much as possible locally to boost the shops.

Amanda chose a dress with a heart-shaped neck, gathers under her breasts, and buttons to below the waist (necessary whilst she was still feeding Luca). The three-quarter sleeves looked elegant without seeming over-dressy. She echoed her mother's vision for the multicoloured flowered black as well as a soft blue. Teresa sent the matching buttons and materials for the waist slips. Jean's fingers were itching to start this work.

Also for a birthday present she included a pair of Italian white sandals with a tiny matching shoulder/handbag and gloves. Amanda and Jean were thrilled with these. When Heather saw the heather material she asked if she might have a coat made in the same cloth. Jean was delighted at this opportunity.

Chapter 6

On the Wednesday before going to Devon, Amanda received her bank statement. The money from the sales and royalties of her three children's books had been paid in. Every six months the amount grew. The books were very popular.

Amanda used this money for presents and when there was an urgent charity need. She and Mark generously supported the Royal Society for the Prevention of Cruelty to Animals. She bought their children handmade shoes. She and Mark continued to buy theirs from Italy. The remaining money she invested in an account which gave interest, but she was able to draw on it when needed.

'Right,' she thought, 'good timing! I will buy materials for new outfits, and treat the family to a small holiday surprise present before we go.'

Joan was going to the garage with Stan and Bob, so Amanda told them she was popping into Brookwell with Luca. Joan offered to go with her.

"No, darling. You carry on. I'm fetching some cash from the bank. Mrs Burton has promised to come with me to help with the pram and doors."

Derby, Amanda's Jack Russell, came with them. She couldn't move without him; she adored him as she had Sparky. She parked the car, and they put Luca in his lightweight pram and went to the bank first. Everyone was pleased to see her and Luca. She had to explain that she couldn't stay out long as she would have to feed Luca. The police in their cars waved to her.

She then went to the bookshop. They hadn't the latest-release detective books she wanted for Mark, Stan, Bob and Luke, but they promised they would have them by the next day and deliver them to the police station. She thanked them, but asked that they be wrapped in plain paper and said that Mr Young senior would collect them. Stan and Bob went to the post office every Thursday for their pensions, and they collected from the bank the petty cash Mrs Burton and she needed.

Next Amanda, Luca and Mrs Burton went to the arts-and-crafts shop and bought Joan a set of embroidery silks of the type she loved to work with. Mrs Burton was looking through designs so they arranged to meet up ten minutes later. She decided to give Adam £12 to spend on art materials, and she thought she would give her children the same amount each.

Amanda said to Luca, "That only leaves you, darling."

She was very happy pushing Luca's pram and she was proud of what she had accomplished. Mark was told that his wife was in Brookwell looking as though she was on a mission!

Mark laughed, "She is preparing for our holiday. Was she on her own?"

"No, she had the baby and Derby."

Stan and Bob had brought the parcel from the bookshop home, so on Saturday morning after breakfast Amanda handed out her holiday presents to them all. She gave Adam his envelope, asking him to buy something for his art, and then gave each of her children their envelopes with money in. They were all thrilled and thanked her for the surprise. The children started discussing what they would buy.

Joshua, Nicola and family travelled by express train to their Devon home, Seaways, on the Thursday to oversee preparations for Amanda and family coming on the Saturday. The house had its own private beach.

Whilst Joshua, Amanda and their families were holidaying in Devon, Teresa and Jonathan went for a few days to the Villa Verona. A pang had gone through Amanda when they asked. Mark realised what she was thinking.

"We will be able to go next year, darling," he said.

She kissed him. "Of course, I am happy with you and our family, sweetheart," she replied.

Nicola, knowing that Amanda required new clothes now that Mark had been promoted, told her she had seen some beautiful materials in a store the year before. Teresa sent her materials, but Nicola thought it would be a change for Amanda to choose some herself. Teresa approved of this and thanked Nicola, saying it would be good for Amanda to choose first-hand. Nicola had brought some latest-design patterns with her in preparation.

She and Susan caught the bus into town on Friday morning. They went to the store. It was busy. Nicola and Susan looked around. An assistant came. She recognised Nicola, who was well known as the co-editor of *Fashion*.

"May I help?" She smiled at her.

"Yes: I need some dress cottons for my sister-in-law. She loves sweet peas. Have you anything in that line?"

"I haven't seen any actual sweet peas. Excuse me a moment, please; I will ask the manageress."

She told Mrs Oliver that "Nicci, the fashion editor," was enquiring about sweet-pea material.

Mrs Oliver asked her customer, who was browsing, to excuse her. She rang the suppliers. Yes, they had some; they could get them to her for the following Monday afternoon. Mrs Oliver went to find Nicola.

She introduced herself and welcomed Nicola to the store. "We are able to obtain sweet-pea materials in 80% cotton, 20% polyester for Monday afternoon, madam. Will this will be of help to you?"

"Thank you, yes. We will come on Tuesday morning. My sister-in-law has a three-month-old baby, so she will not be able to spare much time."

"We would make her comfortable if she needs to feed the baby," Mrs Oliver suggested.

"That's a good thought, thank you, Mrs Oliver. I suggest rolls of pale green, lemon and pale lavender."

"I will arrange this. May I help you further, madam? We have some lovely new dress patterns in."

Thank you, I will have a look. I have brought the latest designs. Lady Amanda likes well-fitted clothes. I have this pattern for a viscose chiffon dress with satin lining."

She showed Mrs Oliver.

"This is beautiful. Please come with me."

"My sister-in-law has red hair."

They had a roll with a pattern of green, lavender, blue and lemon swirls.

"This is gorgeous, Mrs Oliver. Lady Amanda hasn't seen these patterns yet, but I live in hope." She laughed. "Now, I also have in mind for evening wear this pattern. Have you black 93% polyester, 7% elastane with transparent voile for the sleeves?"

"Yes, we have the black."

There was also a vibrant turquoise. Nicola was unsure about this.

"We have the sequins, madam."

"My sister-in-law will not like the sequins, but she may have a little embroidery added at home. Thank you, Mrs Oliver. My daughter and I will browse now, please."

They smiled at each other and Mrs Oliver left.

Susan said, "If Aunt Amanda is coming, Sophie will want to come to look at the sequins."

"Yes," Nicola agreed, laughing, "she will want to come here every day."

They went to look at other cotton materials; there was a lovely selection of ginghams.

"Are you OK, darling?" Nicola asked her daughter.

"I am getting a bit fed up, Mum, but it's OK. I don't have to come next week, do I?"

"No, darling, not if you don't want to. May I have a quick look at what patterns they have here – I promise I won't be long!"

Susan laughed. "It's OK, Mum; I know you want to help Aunt."

Nicola picked out a size-10 pattern in gingham, which Amanda liked. It was sleeveless and button-through with a fitted waist, broad shoulder straps and a heart-shaped neckline. Nicola bought it and asked, "Do you possibly sell wide belts?"

"No, madam; I'm sorry. There is a handbag shop if you turn right when you go out. It's only a short distance."

Nicola thanked her. She and Susan had a quick walk up the street and yes, there were some belts displayed in the window. Nicola was visualising a wide belt and a macramé-frilled hem for the ginghams. This would give Amanda plenty of movement for her support. Also perhaps matching jacket or bolero, for when bare arms weren't appropriate, would be a good idea.

"Come on, Susan darling – let's go and see what your dad and brothers are up to. I'm ready for my lunch."

Susan laughed. "I am also, Mum, as usual."

They ran, hand in hand, back to the car.

As arranged, taxis were available to bring Amanda and her family to Seaways. They had all thoroughly enjoyed the express-train journey, which had taken less than three hours. Luca had offered his pilots, but Amanda had thanked him and explained that the children wanted the train ride like their cousins did.

"Anytime, anywhere, darling!" he promised.

"You know I will ask, darling Luca."

When Amanda had told Nicola they would also be travelling by train, Nicola said, "Only bring the minimum clothing. I will get two extra helpers to keep everything washed and ironed."

Stan and Bob organised the transportation of the trunk and cases.

Arriving at Seaways, they all greeted one another ecstatically. The children, full of joy, ran on to the beach.

When Nicola showed Amanda the suggested patterns for dresses, surprisingly Amanda approved of these new styles.

"I couldn't go flying the kite in these," she teased.

Then she began thinking: 'I will ask Jean to make the floating sleeveless first. I'll bring Mrs Doyle in if necessary; she is always pleased to help Jean. Then I will take Mark to dinner at the Morley for his birthday.' She began to feel excited about this.

Joshua hired a car for Tuesday morning and Nicola drove the short distance into town. Joan, Heather and Sophie came with them; the others chose to go to the beach.

Susan was more than happy to spend time with her cousins. She loved her sister Rose, but thought she was stupid. She said she wouldn't ride a bicycle she might get muscles, and she was always experimenting with make-up and giggling in a silly way on the phone with her friends.

Amanda and Joan were amazed at the rolls of materials with a trailing sweet-pea design. Amanda couldn't believe her eyes; she had never lost her love for sweet peas. She excitedly approved the vanilla and pale lavender. She added the gorgeous pink for the sleeveless and shrug.

"We need contrasting plains for these – especially for the hats, Mrs Oliver," Nicola said.

"I anticipated this."

She smiled and fetched a small book of samples.

They thanked her.

Nicola was encouraged. Amanda had never before shown such interest in her clothes.

Amanda asked the assistant if they delivered to Derbyshire.

"Yes, we can do; we go all over the country."

"Do you sell these materials in Derbyshire and Yorkshire?"

"Not in Derbyshire yet, madam, but we are taking a supply to Sheffield on Friday."

Sophie was impatient, so Joan took her and Heather to look at the sundries, and Sophie found some stick-on patches and strips to cut with sequins on; she was thrilled and couldn't contain her excitement.

Joan was pleased for her but thought with a smile, 'We shall never be away from this shop!'

Sophie counted her money and bought several. All the children had been saving up for this holiday to buy one another presents. Heather bought several pieces of ribbon, braid and buttons from an oddment box. Joan bought some oddments of materials for her patchwork. They were happy looking around to see what else they could find. Heather found some shiny embroidery thread.

They returned to Amanda and Nicola.

Nicola had ordered enough sweet-pea material in the three patterns for dresses with long or three-quarter-length sleeves and a jacket. She also ordered the floaty chiffon and the black evening-dress materials. Nicola had been right: Amanda didn't want the sequins, but she told them, "I know a lady who is expert at machine embroidery. That will suit me better."

Amanda was sat down enjoying a cup of tea and looking at a roll of pure new wool in green, taupe, almond, chocolate and heather mixtures in dogtooth checks for the two-piece pattern Nicola had brought. Amanda liked the skirt, particularly as it had a hem of double frills; this wouldn't cling to her support. Luca was happy, waving his arms and legs up in the air, blowing bubbles and enjoying everyone's attention. Heather asked if she could have a winter coat made from the green mixture. They were all delighted.

The assistant asked Heather, Sophie and Joan if they would like a drink. The three of them had a glass of spring water each. She then brought lengths of soft, pure lamb's wool.

"These are off-cuts, madam; I thought you might want to get

coats and jackets made for your children."

"Yes, thank you."

"I like these – please, Mummy!" Heather told her.

Nicola went with the assistant to look at the other lamb's wool off-cuts; she brought back three more lengths. One was large enough to make Amanda a jacket. Although they were off-cuts they were still expensive. Amanda assured her this was all right and thanked Nicola for thinking of the cost. She told them, laughing, "I am enjoying this. The last time I was in a material shop was before I married, and I now have six children."

They all laughed.

Nicola picked out rolls of checked fine wool and polyester. "These will make Holly and Heather the trousers they favour."

Heather replied, "Oh, yes please, Mummy! I know Holly would like these."

She and Heather liked bib-and-braces overall style, either knee-length or long leg.

Amanda laughed. "I also like the ginghams, and they are cool to wear in the hot weather."

Heather and Amanda chose three colours and a plaid.

Nicola had the pattern of a sleeveless dress (with broad shoulder straps buttoned to the hem and a fitted waist) for Amanda. She loved it.

"This will be perfect for me! Thank you, Nicci."

"I suggest you have a hem of layered macramé trim, darling."

"What is that, Nicci?"

"It's a frilled hem – more movement for your knee support."

"Have you a pattern, please?" she asked the assistant.

"We will have one amongst the skirts, madam."

She quickly brought them a skirt pattern.

Amanda liked it and asked Nicola, "Will Jean know what this is?"

"Yes, darling, but we will take this pattern; it's your size."

Nicola smiled her thanks to the assistant.

Amanda suggested they have the full rolls of gingham and the roll of plaid. "Maybe the boys will like to have shirts made."

"They will, Mummy," agreed Heather.

The assistant then asked, "What about you, Miss Sophie?"

"No, thank you. I like Italian fashion."

They all smiled.

The store was busy, but the assistant gave them her full attention. The manageress came when she was free; they all recognised Nicola's expertise in fashion. They were shown the changing rooms. Amanda took Luca into a private room to feed him. Nicola went with Sophie and Heather to look round more whilst Joan stayed with Amanda.

Mrs Oliver had picked out pieces of different-coloured velvet, suggesting, "They would look well on the collar and pockets for the young lady."

They all approved of this.

"The full rolls you have selected, Lady Amanda, we are able to give a discount on."

Amanda thanked her. She liked a bargain.

The van was delivering on Friday, whilst going to Sheffield. She said they would post the bill.

Amanda thanked Mrs Oliver for all their help. They had all enjoyed themselves. She said that they would be returning to the area at the end of August, so they would certainly visit the shop again.

Mrs Oliver thanked her. "We will save anything suitable for Miss Sophie," she promised.

Amanda laughed.

She asked, "Have you had an opportunity to look at wool, Joan?"

"No, it's all right, darling."

The assistant told them, "We have a supply of new two-tone wools in mixed colours coming in this afternoon."

Amanda suggested to Joan, "Perhaps you would like to come back?"

"Yes."

Sophie piped up: "I would like to come with you, please, Nanny Joan."

"Nanny must have an opportunity to look at the wools, darling. We'll sort this out between us."

"Do you think Daddy will bring me, Mummy?"

They all laughed at this.

"I'm sure he will, darling. You ask him."

They next went to the handbag shop, where Nicola suggested a wide red belt as well as a white one for the ginghams. Amanda happily agreed and bought them.

Nicola always saved her fashion magazines for Sophie; she had brought some for her to look at on holiday. Sophie loved these magazines. She cut pictures out of them and stuck them in books.

The next morning, Mark, Stan and Bob took Joan and Sophie. There was a good bus service. Whilst Stan, Bob and Mark went to the bank for ready cash, they gave Joan and Sophie space to visit the store. They all agreed this would take some time, so they went to look in a shop which sold repossessed goods.

Stan looked in a squashed box and found six boxes of 3-D puzzles and maize balls, which required mental alertness.

The owner asked for £20. "They don't need batteries," he said.

Stan was thinking, 'Are there any more?' He wanted to be fair to all the children.

Mr Lundy said, "Go on – £15, then! I am trying to clear the shop for new supplies."

He and Stan opened the boxes and saw that the balls were undamaged. Stan told him, "I have five grandchildren and we are holidaying with their three cousins. I want to be fair to all of them; have you any more of these, please?" He also didn't want to exclude Rose.

"I will look round, but I doubt it. People won't buy damaged boxes for presents – they usually think the goods are spoilt. But these they are not – just the boxes."

Mark and Bob joined Stan.

Mark said, "The children will love these."

Mr Lundy then brought a box of eight geometric-challenge games and other brain-teasers. "Is £15 OK?" he asked. These also don't need batteries."

Stan paid.

Mark thanked Mr Lundy and told him, "We haven't been in a shop like this before, and I haven't seen these puzzles."

They continued looking round.

Stan suggested, "We need to come back. We had better go and see what the girls are doing."

Mr Lundy said, "Please come back."

They waited outside, and after a while Mark went in and waved to them.

Sophie came running up to him. "Daddy, Daddy!"

He picked her up and asked, "Have you bought the whole store?"

She laughed.

He gave her the weekly pocket money and a little extra for the holiday; then he realised he had made a mistake. They would be here all day!

"We'll come back, if this is OK with your mummy," he promised.

"My daddy is the new Chief Constable of Derbyshire," Sophie proudly told Mrs Oliver.

"Congratulations, sir."

"Thank you. We had better go before you hear all our secrets," he laughed.

Mrs Oliver now understood why she had encountered so much security while trying to locate Chiverton Manor for the delivery men.

"Has Nanny had the opportunity to look at her wool?" Mark asked.

Joan had come up behind him.

"Yes, thank you, Mark. Sophie has been very patient."

He put Sophie down and took the bags from Joan.

Sophie thanked Mrs Oliver and promised she would come again.

Mrs Oliver laughed to herself. When they had left the day before, she had found Sophie some small off-cuts of materials with sparklies on: sequins and rhinestones. Sophie had told her she was going to be a famous actress. She decided to ask the assistants to look round and see what else they could find that Sophie might like. Sophie was such a lovely little personality.

Mrs Oliver went to the door to say goodbye; the family were waiting at a little distance. They all waved. An unexpected pang of loneliness went through her. She would have loved to go back with them.

The family happily went back to the bus stop. The bus this time was a double-decker, so they went upstairs and thoroughly enjoyed the scenery. At Seaways Stan showed them the puzzles. As anticipated, the four boys were thrilled and asked if they could have some for their friends. The three girls asked the same, and so did Luke and Adam.

"I would like to go to that shop," Vincent said.

All the children agreed.

"Yes please! We can go on the bus," said Eric.

Joshua, Luke and Adam said they also would like to go.

They all laughed. They were in Devon in beautiful weather and they all wanted to search round a reclaimed-goods shop!

'Oh well!' thought Joshua. 'It is a change, and travelling on the bus will be an adventure.'

The next morning Mark stayed with Amanda and Luca whilst all the others went shopping. Mark joked, "I hope it's a double-decker bus." He gave his children their pocket money and a bit extra, as he had Sophie.

They all had had a marvellous morning. Joan had her wool, Sophie was given more oddments and loose sequins that Mrs Oliver had found for her, and the others had all bought something from the reclaimed-goods shop!

Knowing Joshua and Nicola had hotelier friends in the area, Stan, whilst on his own with Joshua, asked, "Would you and Nicola like to go out with Amanda and Mark for lunch – perhaps on Friday – with your hotelier friends? Luca would have to go with you, of course, but he is no problem."

"Thanks for that thought, Stan; I had been wondering whether to suggest Mark and Amanda go there for lunch with us to celebrate Mark's promotion. Let me ask Nicola."

After he had discussed it with Nicola, she asked Amanda.

"Thank you, darling," Amanda said. "I am certain Mark will agree with me: we love being with all of you, but we only have these few days this time. Perhaps when we come in August we may do as you suggest."

"Fair enough, darling! August it is, then."

Mark did agree with Amanda, and they thanked Stan for his generous thought. They told Stan it would be arranged for the end of August.

Amanda paid Joan for the beautiful wool she had bought to knit shrugs to match the new sweet-pea-design sleeveless dresses. Joan had also, with Amanda's approval, ordered cones of wools to knit garments on her machine for the children for the autumn and winter. She loved the new colours. There was even some wool with a sparkly thread that Sophie loved. She had also added to their order angora wool in pink and pale lavender.

She didn't go golfing with Stan and Bob that afternoon; she began to knit the lavender/pink mixture wool. She was sure it would look gorgeous when knitted up.

They spent Friday morning on the beach. Luke and Adam didn't go surfing in the afternoon; they swam with Joshua, Mark and all the children whilst Amanda spent time with Nicola. Joan, Stan and Bob went for a game of golf. Everyone was happy and looking forward to their week together at the end of the August holiday. Joshua and Nicola planned to come for their usual month whilst the decorators moved into their home. Teresa and Jonathan and Nicola's parents always joined them for two weeks. Joshua asked Mark if their children would like to come; he thanked him, but said he thought it would be better to wait another year. He knew the children loved holidaying at home. Vincent had told him, "We are enjoying this week, Dad, but it is long enough for us. We will be pleased to get home."

When they arrived home, the dogs were ecstatic, as were the staff. The children ran to see their ponies.

After lunch, Luke went to his fitness studio and Adam went to illustrate his cards. When Amanda had fed Luca, they went into the wood. The children, Stan and Bob were using Stan's navigation system for finding the treasure Mark had hidden.

When Jean saw the materials they had bought, she was thrilled. "There will be enough here to also make Heather a beret," she said.

Chapter 7

The celebration lunch for Mark was on Friday, 15 May. Thankfully it was another beautiful sunny day. The local MP and the other dignitaries had been invited. The Divisional Commander and Mrs Draycott were on holiday abroad with friends. They regretted that they would miss the lunch, but Amanda promised they would invite them to their next musical afternoon. A brilliant entertainment afternoon had been arranged.

The table looked spectacular; members of the Women's Institute had arranged the flowers, as they had for Mark's previous celebration lunch and Amanda's resignation eight years before. The crystal and silver gleamed. Marcos, with his assistant, the Morley chefs and Gerald, had prepared the meal. Extra waiters had been hired from the Devonshire and the Morley. It was such a great occasion that the Morley had closed that lunchtime.

As before, Commissioner Johnson from the Metropolitan Police came in the helicopter with Amanda's parents, Luca, and Dougie (Amanda and Mark's close friend from London Television) and his cameraman.

Joshua and family had come on the express train; they loved travelling that way.

Amanda had, as always, invited representatives of local networks, newspapers and magazines; and they were provided with the same food, set out on outside tables with the Brookwell Male Voice Choir. They all had the greatest respect for Amanda; she helped them and always had fed them. She would have liked them to all eat together, but, even with the very large dining room, there wasn't space. Everyone knew how thoughtful she was and loved her for it. They filmed the table and the guests arriving.

Unfortunately Mrs Blake wasn't well enough to cope with the

crowd and the noise, but now they knew of her illness and all were deeply sorry.

The official photographs were taken outside.

The Reverend Brian said grace.

The food was cooked to perfection as always. Everything fresh from Chiverton and Chatsworth had been used. Amanda's father, as always, had provided the very best of wines. There was a relaxed, friendly atmosphere.

Mr Blake congratulated Mark on his promotion and went on to say, "All the police force has welcomed you. Your abilities, expertise and training as an army colonel have been used and will continue to be. You have won this role on your own merit, but having Lady Amanda at your side is an additional blessing to the community."

Everyone clapped and cheered. Amanda and Mark were both crying.

Mr Blake expressed his personal regret he had had to take early retirement, but he said he was sustained by the thought that it was Mark who was taking over.

Everyone toasted Mark.

The Deputy Chief Constable expressed his thankfulness that Mark had accepted this position. He then expressed, on behalf of everyone in the area, his sorrow at Mrs Blake's illness, and he said they would continue praying for her recovery. He asked everyone to raise their glasses to Mr Blake and wished him, Mrs Blake and their daughter Mildred, who was sat with him, a good quality of life.

Everyone again clapped and cheered.

The Reverend Matthew said a prayer of thankfulness, and a prayer for Mr and Mrs Blake and Mildred. Then he closed with a prayer for Mark, Amanda and their family.

After the meal everyone stretched their legs. The waiters and other staff showed the guests the outdoor pool and changing rooms whilst Amanda fed Luca.

The photographers and cameramen sent their photographs and films back to their offices and studios. Dougie's cameraman sent his film to the BBC, who shared it with London networks. Everyone was interested as Amanda had been a well-known commander, her father was a High Court judge, and her brother was a highly successful and respected lawyer.

They went into the music room. Coffee and drinks were served.

All the children helped Lady Teresa to be hostess in Amanda's absence. Then they prepared for the musical time. Luke set the video camera to record this so that they could all have a copy as before. The cameramen and all the guests joined them. Amanda came in her wheelchair.

It was a wonderful afternoon: Amanda accompanied her father playing his violin, and whilst she was at the piano she and Mark sang a duet. Mark played while their children sang. Rose danced to a tape. The Duke and Lord Richard performed a humorous sketch. The Brookwell Male Voice Choir sang. The volunteers worked through the programme. Everyone taking part did so brilliantly.

Then it was the rock-and-roll time. No one could possibly stay still. To conclude the afternoon Amanda stood with the choir whilst Mark played. They sang 'Be Thou My Vision', and then everyone sang 'Praise My Soul' from words set up on the screen.

Mark stood up. "I thank you all for coming," he said. "I promise you all will receive a video copy of the afternoon. Luke is preparing these as before. Adam and his friends will deliver them this time. (Eight years before, the patrolling police had delivered.)

The guests laughed.

"I thank my wife for organising this day."

Clapping and cheers broke out again.

Mark beckoned the chefs and other staff forward; he had prepared them for this. "Congratulations to all of you for the wonderful meal," he said.

Everyone clapped and cheered them.

Then they all went outside for more casual photographs. Baby Luca was included in these. The coach Mark had hired arrived to take the local guests home. The ones who hadn't been to Chiverton before were discussing how wonderful the afternoon had been, and they said they hoped they would be invited back soon. They were assured that they would be. They talked about the police Saturday afternoons and the parents' kite-flying afternoon, and they discussed the impact this had had on the lives of local families. Mark, with everyone's permission had invited the local newspapers and cameramen, who really appreciated being included. They filmed the Duke running, flying his kite, as well as the families and schoolteachers. Everyone remarked how well mannered all the children were and agreed that they set a good example.

Joshua and family were taken to Chesterton to catch their express train. The Commissioner, Amanda's parents, Luca, and Dougie and his cameraman set off in the helicopter.

Amanda and Mark went swimming with their children.

Holly asked Amanda, "Please, Mummy, may our cousins come to stay with us?"

"Have they asked?"

Vincent told her, "Yes, Mum. We hoped they could come during our week off school."

"Right, but first we need to ask your daddy and Mrs Burton, then Uncle Josh and Aunt Nicola."

Everyone at Chiverton welcomed this proposal.

When Amanda rang Joshua, he asked, "Are they staying for the summer?"

There was laughter at the side of him. His children knew he was joking. He adored them.

"Here's Nicci, who wants a word."

Nicola thanked Amanda. "I think this will be the first of many holidays with you, Amanda," she said.

"I hope so, darling. Our children are maturing."

"May I come up on the Wednesday, if I am allowed by my lot?"

"You will be very welcome, darling."

Amanda rang off and asked the children, "Will you all help to prepare their rooms and organise the days?"

Jonathan and Teresa, Nicola and Joshua and the children stayed in en-suite bedrooms at Christmas and the occasional stays. Although the children were roughly eight years older than Amanda and Mark's, of course they all got on together very well. For the twins and triplets it was like having older brothers and sisters.

Amanda asked the decorators to come and freshen up the rooms.

When she and Mark were having their soak in the bath, Mark, as always, massaged her damaged leg. They discussed the children coming to stay.

Mark said, "We have to reconcile ourselves, sweet, to the fact that our children are growing up."

"Yes," Amanda agreed, "it has to be. We must let them take responsibility for making sure their cousins have what they need in their rooms and for co-ordinating together a daily programme."

Lady Teresa rang Amanda and Mark to congratulate them on the celebration lunch.

Amanda told her, "The children and Josh and Nicola have arranged between them to come here for the Spring Bank Holiday week. They are growing up too quickly, Mum."

"That's what your dada and I thought about you and Josh, darling."

"We have given them the responsibility of preparing the rooms."

"Good."

Teresa broke off to speak to Jonathan.

"Your dada wants a word, darling."

"Congratulations, darling! The lunch was an outstanding success. Well done!"

"It was teamwork, Dada."

"Now, Amanda, your mum has just briefed me about the children coming to stay with you. They are all maturing fast, and we are proud of you all for encouraging them to be independent. Society being what it is now, these qualities of maturity and independence will hold them in good stead. You and Josh were independent and neither of you have turned out too bad."

Amanda laughed. "Darling Dada, thank you," she said. "I feel better now."

"Be in touch soon!"

In the background Teresa could also be heard saying goodbye. Amanda, not for the first time by any means, thanked God for the way her parents encouraged her.

Nicola texted Amanda: 'I need to speak to you urgently, darling. Rose has asked if she may go with one of her friends and parents round the Greek islands at the end of May.'

Amanda rang her. "Of course, darling, we will all miss her, but she is nearly sixteen years old. It is a wonderful opportunity for her."

When it was a suitable time, Amanda broke this news to her family. She expected Sophie to be upset because she had been preparing for Rose coming; she had bought her the latest magazines and cut pictures of ballet dancers and stuck them in a book and put posters on her bedroom wall.

As anticipated, Sophie was heartbroken.

Amanda explained, "She is nearly sixteen years old, darling. She is a young lady. It is a wonderful opportunity for her to holiday in Greece. The others are coming, and Aunt Nicola is also coming on the Wednesday."

Mark took Sophie for a walk.

Amanda asked the family, "What can we do to cheer Sophie up?"

They all knew how much Sophie had looked forward to Rose coming and they were aware of the preparations she had made, so they understood why she was so upset.

"We could ask her to dance for us, Mum."

"What a wonderful idea, Vincent! Well done!"

Everyone echoed that.

"Make it special. I will play, and will you all please take photographs?"

They promised they would. Luke promised to film it. Heather suggested they present her with a bouquet from the garden.

"She will love that," replied Amanda.

The children went to find her and their father. They asked Sophie, and she was thrilled. The dance was arranged for before their Saturday afternoon swim. Luke always came home from his fitness studio to help Mark with this.

Amanda and Sophie practised in private.

Sophie wore a frilly dress and danced beautifully. The other children photographed her, and Luke filmed. They all applauded whilst she curtsied, and when Vincent presented her with the flowers she looked radiant.

Mark teased her: "You will have to get used to this when you are a famous actress."

"Oh, Daddy, I love you."

She climbed on to his knee and Mark cuddled her. She was only five years old, but he was aware that she and the other children would have to get used to being disappointed when things didn't always turn out the way they wanted.

Chapter 8

On the Tuesday early evening news, Mrs Hudson, the local MP, gave out the information that Mr Tony Searston would reveal the new owners of Searstons on the coming Thursday. The billboards advertised this.

Mark, with respect, had previously informed the local MP and dignitaries in confidence.

Mr Tony Searston began: "I have great pleasure in revealing that the new owners are Lady Amanda Young and her brother, Mr Joshua Dansie, a lawyer in London. They have bought the factory."

There were loud cheers and clapping.

"I'm staying on for a few weeks to help in any way I can. Mr Adam Young is the office manager. My son is going to be employed part-time also, as an advisor. The machines are going to be updated. Six new ones have been ordered. The car-making unit is being reopened, and we already have an order."

Cheers broke out again.

It was Mark, after discussing with Amanda and Joshua, who had ordered the car. He asked for a ten-seater with opening roof and provision (including an air vent) for the dogs. Now that the children were growing up, he thought they could use this car to go out as a family at weekends and during holidays. They could also take it to the local Chatsworth House shows, where Holly and Vincent had entered the gymkhana for the last two years. They could all take the car to other shows in the area.

Mr Searston continued: "It goes without saying that we are most grateful that Lady Amanda and Mr Dansie have bought this factory. As you know, with the economy in recession we have not been able to produce quickly enough using the old machines. We lost orders and had to lay off members of the workforce. The good news is that they will now be reinstated, thanks to the new ongoing orders for aeroplanes in Italy. Again we thank Lady Amanda for this."

Surprisingly, Mr Searston broke down at this point. His son joined him. He also was upset.

Simon laughed. "Sorry. It's just that such a weight has been taken off our shoulders! Perhaps you understand how we mentally suffered when we had to make redundancies. Lady Amanda and Mr Dansie have both had to make sacrifices to buy this factory and make the necessary improvements. I will be in trouble for telling you this, but I think you ought to know and appreciate the commitment they have made."

Simon then told them, "My dad and I have pledged we will do everything to help them. Mr Dansie is a busy lawyer in London with a wife and four growing children, and Lady Amanda has a large family and is now supporting her husband in his role as our Chief Constable. The reason the takeover was brought about in secret is that when we began negotiations her husband had just been promoted and Lady Amanda insisted she didn't want any publicity that would distract attention from his accomplishment."

Cheers erupted again, as Simon then also broke down.

"The factory will be closed for the spring Bank Holiday as usual," he continued, "and the following week it will remain closed for repainting and the six new machines will be installed. John and I will oversee all of this. All the workers, including those who have been reinstated, will continue to be paid while the factory is closed."

The interview ended with both their wives comforting them.

The local MP and other dignitaries gave an interview which expressed their support and thankfulness that the factory was saved.

John had a word with the reporters: "I think it would be good to let everyone know that Mr Tony Searston has given all his workmen, including the reinstated ones, a very generous bonus out of his own pocket."

They thanked John for that information.

He asked, "Please don't reveal that it was me who told you."

They laughed and promised.

After everyone had stretched their legs, they met up for afternoon tea, which was served at the tables outside. March and April had been sunny and very warm. They had the blessing of another very warm day after several days of heavy rain and wind. The children helped to pass the food around. There was great joy amongst them all.

The Messrs Searston interview had a profound effect on the community. They knew Lady Amanda was a millionaire, but for her to have given so generously – well!

The interview with Amanda and Joshua was shown the following day in the early evening. They had been filmed at Chiverton that afternoon. Both were dressed casually, and the dogs were running about.

Joshua opened with, "We thank Messrs Searston for their remarks. We also are very grateful that they, John and Gavin, are helping us to set up this new business. My sister and I have made sacrifices, but it has been a blessing for us. My sister has six children so far [laughter from the cameramen and reporters], and I have four children, full stop [laughter again]. We have their future to consider. Lady Amanda and I have wonderful parents who wisely invested money for both of us."

Then the camera went on Amanda. "Yes, we do have wonderful parents and they taught us Christian values. I also thank them for helping us. I take this opportunity to say how grateful I am to have been my Aunt Sophie's heiress. When I came here to recuperate eight years ago I fell in love with my husband at first sight."

The cameras panned across to Mark, who stood at the side cuddling Luca, surrounded by his children and more dogs. He was looking at Amanda with adoration.

"I also fell in love with this community," Amanda continued. "I knew I had come home!"

She was interrupted by cheers and clapping.

She laughed. "We have made sacrifices, but my brother and I have been truly blessed in having parents who gave us money they had invested for us. My brother was Aunt Melissa's heir; she was the elder twin of our Aunt Sophie. We have been, I say again, greatly blessed, not just with love but with financial security. Therefore, because our family have provided for us, my brother and I are following in their footsteps and we are using our inheritances in honour of them to help others. Through my aunt I have known Count Luca Villani and his family since I was very young. We know he and his sons will provide us with ongoing orders." There were cheers again, and Amanda laughed. "My brother needed approval from his wife, and I needed approval from my husband. Also we had to check with our expert advisors and our parents. Last but not least, much prayer went into it. We are also very grateful for Messrs Searston's promise of support. We are aware of our responsibility. My brother is a highly respected lawyer, and you will appreciate that I didn't get to be a Metropolitan commander by taking my responsibilities lightly. You may rest assured you can trust us. We wouldn't like my husband to arrest us!"

Great laughter broke out.

Mark was laughing and thinking, 'Good girl!'

"I end with grateful thanks to God for all his blessings."

Everyone clapped and cheered.

Nicola, Mark and all the children and dogs joined them. Mark and Amanda put their arm round each other. A close-up was taken of Luca in Mark's other arm. He was chuckling. Nicola was asked to pose for the photographers. She laughingly agreed. They knew she had been a fashion model. The networks rushed off to get these interviews into the early evening news. The photographers asked for casual photographs and sent these back to their offices.

The reporters then asked Amanda to tell them about her aunts.

She told them, "My Aunt Sophie, Contessa Gambetti, had only been married for two weeks when Vincent, her husband, instantly died after his motorcycle skidded on ice. He adored racing his motorcycles, but he promised her he would be careful. They had everything to live for; they both wanted a family; they adored each other. In her grief and loneliness she rebuilt her life and learnt to run his businesses. As you know, she helped the local glassware factory. My brother's benefactor, Aunt Melissa, had a fashion store in Italy and bought a shop in London which over the years she built up into the prestigious business which is Mason's. Joshua and I now share this business, through our inheritance, along with our mum. Two managers and our mum run this business. Our aunts were committed business ladies. This is why we are taking the responsibility of this factory, bought with their money, very seriously. My brother and I are also very grateful to our parents for releasing investments which they set up for us. I am looking forward to getting to know the workforce. I will not be remote. However, as I said previously, my husband is the first priority in my life and then my children."

They all thanked her for this. She invited them to have another drink, but they excused themselves to get back to their offices. They knew she would keep them informed of any developments now that the news was revealed.

Letters and cards of appreciation poured in for Amanda and Joshua. Gifts also were sent. Hilary Land was so devastated by the thought of how she had blown it with Adam by being too pushy that she went back to Huddersfield.

Simon, John, Gavin and Adam held a meeting for the machinists.

John opened with, "We have selected twelve men to operate the new machines." He told them the names. "Whilst the old machines are being restored we will work a double shift. This will continue, for a while at least, as we need to deal with the new orders quickly. You will all be given training when we reopen after the holiday. We will alternate the shifts weekly. Naturally, the evening shift will be unsociable hours, so you get more pay. Gavin or I will be with you. Have you any questions?"

A lady packer asked, "Shall we be working the two shifts?"

"No, Maureen, but thanks for that question."

Adam printed a rota out for the noticeboard.

One man spoke up: "We are all very grateful to Lady Amanda and Mr Dansie for buying this factory. We all thought and dreaded that it would close. We will all do our very best to give satisfaction as we have over the years for Mr Tony and Mr Simon Searston, whom we thank for being great employers. We would like to have this put on record."

John thanked them, and he promised to arrange this.

They broke for coffee.

With the recession, and new cars not being made, orders poured in from garages and owners for parts to restore cars in use. The factory managed to regain the order it had lost.

To celebrate this new beginning for him, Adam booked Sunday lunch for his 'gang' at the farm shop and answered their questions about his new job with Dansie & Young. He apologised for not telling them before; but, having heard his sister-in-law's interview, they understood her wish not to reveal news of the factory deal until after his brother's promotion. They all congratulated him and said how pleased they were for him. They realised that this was a new opportunity for him to use the skills he had worked hard for in school and university.

Next Adam told them about the unit he had bought and how now he was renting it to the owner of the stenography business.

They celebrated with glasses of champagne at the farm shop. Adam decided he would tell them another time about his mum remarrying.

"Perhaps you and Joshua need to consider having apprentices trained for the machines," Stan suggested to Amanda.

"Yes, Dad, that's a good idea. I'll ask Josh about this."

When she had his permission, she faxed John about it, and he and Gavin agreed. Adam contacted the local college. Yes, they had space for two apprentices to begin a four-year course in the coming September. During the first year, the course would be five days a week, thereafter reducing to one day and one evening a week.

Adam advertised the two apprenticeships and stressed the need for references and health checks. One young lady applied! This caused problems. What should they do about this? They interviewed her and they were all impressed by her school qualifications and her interest in engineering. She had for a few years helped her father with his car and her brothers with their motorcycles. They employed her and a local young man, and the college was pleased to receive the two applications for the engineering course.

Adam gave this news to the local papers, and he said that they would be advertising for more apprentices the following year. When experienced mechanics enquired if there was a vacancy, Adam recorded their names, expertise and addresses. He promised that if anything came up, he would contact them. He designed the company's new stationery.

Simon and John came to Chiverton every Thursday morning to meet with Amanda and Adam. Adam faxed Joshua with every detail and always asked for his advice or approval. This was a good working arrangement, and Amanda also had conversations with them both about the business.

All was going well with the two shifts, and the men were grateful for the steady flow of work.

Simon raised the question, "What are we doing about the car-making unit?"

"We need to go ahead with this," John advised. "Some of the experienced engineers who have applied had expertise in this work. We only need to take on two of them at the moment."

"That's fine with me," laughed Amanda. "The sooner you begin work on my husband's car the better."

They all agreed.

"When we have Mr Dansie's approval we will contact the applicants and also advertise. A bird in the hand is worth two in the bush."

"Whatever does that mean?" Amanda asked.

"Better be safe than sorry, ma'am!"

"OK," she laughed.

"It would be brilliant if you could come to the factory, Lady Amanda. It's very noisy in the workshop, but quiet in my office. There would be privacy for you to feed Luca," Adam said. He always used her title in work situations. He was her employee.

"Yes, I would love to come; I promised I would not be remote."

It was set up for Amanda, Stan and Bob to go, and Joan agreed to look after Luca. The afternoon shift came in to meet Amanda. Her visit was a great success, and they all appreciated the interest she took in their work. She promised to return soon.

Simon took her into the packing room and introduced the female workforce. Some, like many of the men, had worked there for thirty years. Everywhere was clean. She then went into the canteen; meals were not cooked, but there was a coffee-and-tea machine. Drinking water was also available. She was presented with a beautiful bouquet.

Simon then took her to meet the office staff, and Margaret asked if she would like a coffee?

"I prefer tea, please."

They went with Adam into his office, where Luca was happily sleeping, and Margaret and Simon brought in trays with beautiful bone-china cups, saucers and plates with a blue harebell design. Amanda was thrilled with these. Sandwiches were offered and then cake. They all tucked in.

Then Amanda was given privacy to feed Luca, as Adam had promised. She told the office staff she would return soon. She had meant it when she said she would not be remote. They were all pleased.

Vincent and Holly said they would like to go with her next time. Amanda suggested they could all go during the August school holiday.

Eric asked, "May I also go, Mummy. I will work for you when I am older."

"Thank you, darling." He came to stand against her, and she asked, "May I give you a cuddle?"

He laughed, "That's OK at home, Mummy."

To celebrate the success of the factory, Amanda invited the Messrs Searston, John, Gavin, Jack (the solicitor) and all their families for Saturday lunch. Joshua was unable to come because of a prior commitment, but he reassured Amanda that she should go ahead.

Mark approved of this. "The families will be more relaxed with this smaller fellowship. They know Dad and Bob," he said.

Amanda recognised the logic of this.

They had a wonderful relaxed time and appreciated Amanda inviting them. After Amanda had fed Luca, they all went for a walk through the wood.

Teresa shared with her husband: "I do admire Amanda for the way she involves the children in giving hospitality. I regret I didn't do that with her and Joshua."

"Darling, our meals were in the evenings and more official. Amanda's are lunches – different timings and less formal."

She kissed him. "Thank you, my precious. You are right as usual."

He hugged her and they laughed.

"Amanda has come a long way in being a hostess," he said.

"Yes, she is first class."

Chapter 9

When the news of the factory was widely broadcast, a friend of Lord Ian (Andrew's father) contacted him telling him he had a very dilapidated 1920s Bugatti Type 35 racing car in his workshop. It had been there for years as he had been unable to spare time repairing it. He was now retiring. Jeremy and his wife were keen golf players, and they were selling up and buying a small golf business with a house. Mrs Crosslie had put her foot down and said they would not be taking all their "rubbish" with them! Jeremy asked Ian to contact Chiverton and ask if they wanted to have it and any other bits and pieces; all they needed to do was to collect them.

Stan and his friends were thrilled to bits about this. They made arrangements with the local garage to fetch it to the workshop, where there was a spare inspection pit. Stan and his car pals followed.

The car was a sorry sight, as some of Andrew's cars had been, but they were all excited.

"Bugatti cars are worth a lot of money, Mr Crosslie."

"This one needs to be restored before it is of any value. My uncle gave it to me as it is. I think it is impossible to get parts, though admittedly I haven't seriously tried. You are very welcome to take all the bits and pieces with you – otherwise they will just go for scrap. I would rather you have them if they will be useful to you."

Stan accepted the offer with delight, and Mr Crosslie invited them to look round and take anything they wanted. They all supervised the crane loading the Bugatti on to the trailer, and when it was safely in place they went back for the boxes of parts.

Mrs Crosslie invited them to have lunch with them; they thanked her but said they needed to get back as the truck was needed.

She told them, "I am so grateful to you for taking all this."

Her housekeeper brought them coffee. She enquired about Lady Amanda and family.

They all thanked the Crosslies, and Stan asked Mr Crosslie, "If we are able to restore it, would you like it returned?"

"No. Enjoy it or, if you sell, give the money to your favourite charities."

They all shook hands and thanked him again.

As they travelled back, Fred said, "We never know what is coming next since Lady Amanda came up here."

They all agreed and they couldn't wait to find out what repairs the car needed.

"It will be a marvellous car to take to Chatsworth, even if it takes years – as some of the other cars have," Stan said.

When they had offloaded the Bugatti into the workshop, Stan said, "Come on – let's go and have a drink and meal in the Devonshire. I'll treat you."

They quickly cleaned themselves!

Stan was informed of a garage in Sheaf where they bought and repaired antique cars. He hoped they could obtain parts for this Bugatti if they couldn't make the parts themselves. Both Luke and Adam wanted this car. Stan told them, "No way!"

When they had cleaned the Bugatti up, Stan suggested they go to look at the garage in Sheaf.

Joan went with them on the bus. They often used the buses; they had good services from Brookwell and it encouraged others to travel this way.

Fred joked, "We are helping to save the environment!"

Arriving at the garage, they were all thrilled to see the antique cars on display. The owner joined them, introduced himself as Barrie Croft, and asked if they were interested in any of the cars.

Stan told him the cars they had and how they had obtained them eight years before; now they had been given a 1920s Bugatti.

Barrie was excited: "A Bugatti! May I buy it?"

Stan laughed. "Sorry, we are hoping to repair it and enter it in the Chatsworth Rally eventually."

Barrie then told them he had heard of this event, and he said he would like to enter it too.

Fred gave him details and told him how to apply.

Barrie asked them to call him by his first name; they agreed to use first names all round. They were all very comfortable with one another. He offered them a drink, which they accepted with pleasure. He took them into his office.

"I have retired from the police force," Barrie said. "My wife died three years ago. My family are all happily married with families of their own. I have always been interested in old cars, so I have taken the opportunity of buying this garage. Now that I live here, I am making lots of new friends through the cars."

They all introduced themselves. When Stan told him he and Bob were retired police inspectors, Barrie jumped up and shook their hands. He asked, "Which area?"

"Derbyshire."

"Derbyshire? That is where Commander Dansie's husband has been promoted to Chief Constable, isn't it?"

They all laughed.

Stan explained, "The Chief Constable is my eldest son."

"Congratulations! You must be very proud of him."

"Yes; I am also proud of my other two sons. Luke is a fitness trainer in the force, and he also has his own fitness studio. Adam, my youngest, has a Cambridge masters degree in business studies and economics."

Barrie was overwhelmed. "Well done, Stan! You are very God-blessed. Their mother must also be very proud."

"She is, but unfortunately we are divorced."

Barrie didn't know how to reply to that. "I'm from Hampshire," he said. He smiled at Joan.

Joan, for the first time in her life, experienced a pull of attraction.

Stan then told him, "Joan is Lady Amanda's close friend."

Barrie's telephone rang. He excused himself. They went outside and waited. Eventually, he came rushing up to them and they all went to look at his cars. They were all impressed. In the workplace there were some old cars waiting to be renovated, and the shelves were stacked with parts. Barrie introduced his two workmen.

"I would love you to have lunch with me, but unfortunately I have an appointment with the dentist." He laughed. "May I come soon to view the Bug?"

They all assured him he would be welcome. Fred told him where it was, and after ringing Dave they arranged to meet there on Thursday morning at 10.30 and then have lunch at the Devonshire. Barrie was hoping to have a car accepted in the Chatsworth Rally.

Stan told Mark about this meeting; Mark made security enquiries about Barrie. His reputation was exemplary and everything he had told them was true.

When they met up at the garage, Barrie asked, "Was Joan unable to come?"

Stan told him, "She is joining us for lunch." He had booked a table at the Devonshire.

Barrie was thrilled with the Bug, as he called it. "I have been online and found a possible help in Northampton," he said. "They are sending me a manual. I am positive we will be able to obtain parts if between us we cannot make them. Here is a toy clockwork model." Laughing, he gave Stan a small box.

Stan thanked him and said, "Vincent and Eric will love this."

After a good lunch they went back to the garage. Barrie had to leave them, but they all promised they would keep in touch.

Stan mentioned to Amanda that he thought Joan and Barrie were attracted to each other. She was thrilled, but she had a moment of apprehension that change would be on the way. She rebuked herself for this selfish thought, and consoled herself by recalling that Joan had always been part of her life. Joan was adored by all who knew her.

"Mark, I asked Joan if she would like to invite Barrie to lunch, but she refused, saying they were just good friends."

"Now, Amanda, you had me believe years ago that she and Dad would marry."

"Sorry – I will now keep my nose out." She laughed. "I don't want Joan to feel intimidated about asking her friends here."

"Her Women's Institute friends come, sweetheart. You should be a matchmaker," he teased.

"Right, I promise I will never interfere again."

Mark quietly told her, "You were not wrong, but Dad felt he was still married to Mum, and Joan said she was too set in her ways. I am, and always have been, very thankful that Dad has her and Bob; and I'm grateful to you too, darling, for helping him to rebuild his life."

Luke and Adam searched the Web and found 1:18 scale die-cast models of three of the cars Stan and his pals had restored; they bought these plus showcases for their father as a birthday present. He was absolutely thrilled, and this began a new interest for him and the family. Vincent, Eric and Holly bought toy models from their local shop.

Chapter 10

After Teresa spoke at Chiverton about how proud she was, and always had been, of Joshua and Amanda. They had never caused her or their father any problems. How God-blessed they were to have such beautiful grandchildren! In contrast, Luca sat in his Italian garden with a glass of wine, reflecting regretfully on his own life.

He had had three failed marriages, which had cost him a lot of money, and still did. He and his ex-wives were still friends; at least that was one bright light. If his sons had not squandered so much money on their lavish lifestyles, they could have been billionaires by now. "Ah well," he sighed, "we cannot go back; we can only go forward from now.

Luca invited Lorenzo, Lorenzo's wife Christiana, and Santorini to dinner.

He told them, "Amanda and Joshua are going forward with buying the Derbyshire factory with the help of their parents."

They were pleased.

"The factory will provide the parts we need for the aeroplane business," Santorini said. "We will provide them with plenty of work, and when others know it is Amanda's factory they will order."

Luca and Lorenzo agreed.

Lorenzo and Santorini had never known their father to be so serious.

Luca went on: "I have been reflecting on my life. I feel I have been such a failure to you both. Amanda and Joshua's parents have always set them a good example, but I have not done this for you. I deeply regret this. Last Friday afternoon was a time of letting go of the past and beginning a new chapter. Mark has been promoted to Chief Constable of Derbyshire."

They were overwhelmed at this. Santorini said, "Amanda is the perfect wife for him in this role."

"Yes, but he has gained this honour on his own merit," said Luca. They all went quiet, knowing this was so.

"Now back to us," Luca went on: "I have squandered money – you have squandered money – I regret my three failed marriages."

Santorini and Lorenzo were wondering what was coming next. Was he going to disown them?

"Now we and Amanda have bought Signor Rossi's business and we are going to have Amanda and Joshua's factory doing work for us. Out of respect for Lady Teresa and Lord Dansie we need to begin to be responsible citizens. We should learn from this family. I am changing my ways. We do not have to be miserable. Look at our beloved Amanda – she is full of hope and joy. She could have gone the wrong way when her fiancé was killed and her knee was shattered. Her leg isn't perfect – she suffers much discomfort – but has she blamed anyone?"

They agreed she had not.

Santorini spoke: "Yes, Papa, we understand what you are saying. We need to take responsibility for our own actions. Signor Rossi spent almost a lifetime building up his business; we need to build on his reputation."

Christiana spoke: "I would like to be involved in this business instead of spending my time and money on the latest fashions and other trivial things. I will try to be more like Amanda. I will try to support you more. Together we can teach our children to be disciplined and responsible citizens."

Lorenzo hugged her.

Santorini admitted he had squandered money; when his relationships had ended he had bought them expensive presents. "I need to settle down now," he said.

Luca thanked them.

Lorenzo and Santorini told him he had been a good papa. He thanked them again, but stated, "I will now be a better papa and a better grandpapa."

Santorini said, "Now we will have more contact with Amanda and Josh. We will be more in touch with them."

"You should see how well behaved all Amanda and Mark's

children are. They love simple pleasures, such as flying their kites and playing in the grounds and wood – even Sophie, who has Italian genes and is going to be a famous actress," Luca told them.

They laughed.

Santorini asked, "Is it possible for all of us to visit Chiverton?"

Lorenzo agreed. "Our children must behave, though," he said with a laugh.

Then Luca laughed and told them, "If they don't, Holly will throw them about with her martial-arts skills!"

Santorini winced. "Amanda was the same at that age," he said.

They all laughed again, then fell silent.

Santorini had planned to go on to a nightclub, but he decided against it. Instead he decided to go to his gym for a workout. They thanked Luca for the evening. He thanked them.

When they had left, he went into his office and studied again the contract they had with Sergio Rossi. He threw it down and texted Antonia, Lorenzo and Santorini's mother, his first wife. They kept in contact, as he did with his other two ex-wives. She had never stopped loving him, despite her hurts and the humiliation he had caused by his affairs. She hadn't wanted to divorce him, but she knew the only way they would remain friends was to let him go.

Antonia rang back: "I am at Gina's, darling. Is it urgent?"

"Yes. Please, *cara mia*, I need to speak with you. Are you able to come now?"

"Yes, darling. Are you ill?"

"No, *cara*, I have never felt better. I need to speak to you about our sons and family. Shall I fetch you?"

"I have my car."

She excused herself to her friends. They knew she still loved Luca and would do anything for him.

Luca was waiting for her. They embraced. He made her comfortable on the patio overlooking the garden. He poured her a glass of her favourite wine. With her permission, he lit a cigar. He always asked. She waited patiently.

"Lorenzo, Christiana and Santorini have dined with me. We have had an in-depth discussion. We, as you know, will be having parts for the aeroplanes made in Derbyshire, in Britain. Lady Amanda and her brother are buying the components factory."

Antonia waited again.

"I regret what I have done in my life, *cara mia*: how I must have hurt and humiliated you; how I have squandered money; that I haven't been a good example to our sons. They have squandered money too."

"Darling," she interrupted, "are you short of money?"

He laughed. "No, *cara*."

"What is it, then, Luca?"

"We are going to turn over a new leaf, as they say."

"What does that mean?" she queried.

"Be more responsible, mature adults. We have the example of Amanda and her family and now we have a connection with the area where she and her family live. We need to be worthy of her."

Antonia told him, "You are a good man, Luca, but you lost your way, didn't you? Contessa Sophie didn't like the way you were going."

"No," he admitted, "but there is something about Chiverton Manor and that community which is so good and wholesome. Amanda and Mark's children love the simplicity of the country life. They are mischievous, but they are sound and responsible for their age. Amanda is a millionaire, but she hasn't spoilt them; they are surrounded by love and security. Sophie has Italian genes."

"I would love to meet them, Luca."

"Yes, we will make a date; we could go for the day. A Saturday would be best for Amanda and Mark, I think."

Antonia had a highly successful jewellery store she had built up over the years. "I could be free whenever you arrange, darling."

"Would you like another drink, *cara*?"

"I would like you to take me to your bed."

"I thought you would never ask," he teased.

She knew he was clean – he had always used protection.

Afterwards, he asked, "Am I too late in asking you to make a new start with me, *cara mia*?"

"No, but you are emotional just now, Luca. Let's take it one step at a time. I couldn't bear to be hurt again."

He gathered her close.

Amanda and Mark welcomed them to Chiverton. To help Gerald she had hired waiters and two chefs who specialised in Italian cooking.

The children were excited at the Italians' coming; their Italian was getting very fluent, as was the French and German which they learnt at school. Amanda and Mark also conversed with them in these languages when they were alone.

Antonia had bought (with Amanda's permission) a beautiful jewelled watch for each of the girls and latest-technology watches for each of the two older boys. She had bought the same for her other grandchildren. They were all thrilled. She had bought Luca a mobile for his cot. She had bought a lovely brooch for Joan, a dainty watch with tiny sweet peas on its face for Amanda and for Mark gorgeous gold cufflinks.

They were particularly enchanted with Sophie and Luca, but they treated all the children the same. They were fascinated by Heather's pale auburn hair in her long plait. Christiana had, with Amanda's permission, brought Sophie Italian children's fashion catalogues.

After lunch the twins and triplets sang in Italian whilst Amanda played the piano. All the children then ran to see the ponies. They got the bikes out and took turns to ride up the path to the top field. Then they freewheeled down, shouting at the top of their voices! The Italian children were getting too daring and overexcited, so Mark rounded all of them up and they went into the wood with the dogs. Before long Lorenzo's children were climbing trees and swinging dangerously on the branches.

Mark quietly asked Amanda, "Are we having them for a week?"

They both laughed.

After afternoon tea they returned to London. The day had been a resounding success, and thankfully there were no broken bones or worse! The children had bonded and were going to write to one another.

On the way back, Antonia told her sons, Lorenzo and Santorini, "I am releasing money for you to put into your new business. As Lady Teresa said, 'Why wait until I am dead?' " The two young men were happy at this – the money would greatly help them –

but they were happier at their parents' obvious new closeness. They discussed what a wonderful example Amanda and Mark's children had been; Antonia went back with Luca.

Luca invited Antonia for a few days to his London apartment; she accepted with delight. He contacted Teresa and asked her to recommend a couple of shows Antonia would like. Teresa invited them to dinner.

She and Antonia loved one another as sisters. This was an eye-opener for Jonathan. Most of the time he forgot Teresa was Italian.

He began to think. She adored him, he knew, and their children and grandchildren, and was always available for them, sacrificing at times her commitment to Mason's. She always gladly gave hospitality to his colleagues. He decided he would take her to Italy as a surprise when he had a long weekend free. He also thought he would ask Luca and Antonia to dine with them on the Saturday evening and go to the opera if they were free. Also, he decided to take Teresa to Antonia's shop and buy her a piece of jewellery.

When he told Teresa about taking her, "Where are we going?" she asked.

"I want it to be a surprise," he answered. "You know I have always adored you, my precious wife, but at times I have neglected you."

She felt his forehead and laughed. "It feels normal," she said.

He pulled her on to his knee and silently cuddled her. She understood. She also was reflecting.

Jonathan was still very handsome; he still had a head of thick, red, wavy hair. He now had a slight stoop, but he was still very charismatic. She knew, and had always known, he was surrounded by attractive females, and she knew some of them would offer him temptation in order to further their careers, but she also knew he had been faithful to her. He would never encourage them. She held him very tight.

Later, when she told Amanda and Joshua that their father was taking her away for the weekend as a surprise, they were thrilled.

When Luca and Antonia came to Teresa and Jonathan for dinner for the second time during their week in London, Luca told them how much their family was now influencing him, his sons and family. He said that the children were now being brought up to enjoy the simple pleasures of life.

Jonathan agreed. "That is how Teresa brought Amanda and Josh up."

Teresa broke in: "You brought them up too, sweetheart."

Teresa took Antonia and Luca to Mason's. Antonia was particularly interested in their jewellery department.

On the Thursday Luca had a meeting arranged for the airline business. Teresa booked Antonia and herself into a full-day massage and top-to-toe beauty treatment. The four of them planned to go to the ballet that evening.

Luca told Jonathan, "We have the most beautiful ladies in the world on our arms, haven't we, Jonathan?"

He agreed.

Antonia and Teresa laughed. They were pleased. They had both looked after their figures with diet and exercising. They were photographed by the press, who asked Luca if he and his ex-wife were together again. They all just smiled at them.

Chapter 11

"We will need extra help preparing for our extended family's needs," Amanda told them.

"Eddie's sister has almost completed her cookery course at the college. She is a good kid; perhaps she can help. He did mention a while ago that she could do with a part-time job. I forgot about it," Adam told Amanda. Eddie was one of their gardeners.

"I'll tell Gerald and Mrs Burton. May I leave it with you, Adam, to find out when she is able to come and see us?"

"Of course, Amanda."

An interview was set up. Anne impressed Amanda, Gerald and Mrs Burton very much; she was a quiet, well-mannered young lady. Her appearance was very clean and she had short, scrubbed nails. Mrs Burton knew the family.

Amanda showed her the children's menus she always asked for, depending on the ingredients they had available in the garden and greenhouse.

Amanda, with approval from Gerald and Mrs Burton, asked Anne to come for the week. She said she could come for 7 a.m. and stay all day, as she was needed. Gerald and Mrs Burton welcomed that. A wage was agreed.

Anne thanked Amanda and told her she would be grateful for the money and, most importantly, the training. "If you need me any time at weekends, ma'am, or evenings, I will be pleased to come," she said.

Amanda thanked her.

"May I ask you something, ma'am?"

"Yes, Anne?"

My friend Jayne is training to be a nanny at the same college as me. She wondered if she might come with me for the week to do any washing or to help with cleaning the rooms."

"That's a good thought, Anne," said Mrs Burton, who also knew Jayne and her family.

"She had better come and see us, Anne," said Amanda. "Ask her to contact Mrs Burton."

Anne left. Gerald and Mrs Burton were satisfied and they said it would be useful that she lived nearby.

"As you are aware, now that my husband is the Chief Constable we will have to do more entertaining when I have weaned Luca. If you both approve of Anne after the week, perhaps we could offer her a job when she has finished college?" Amanda asked Gerald and Mrs Burton.

They approved of this idea.

Then Mrs Burton told Amanda, "Adele is pregnant, ma'am, so she will be leaving."

Amanda was pleased for Adele and her husband. "Is she able to work just now?" she asked.

"Yes, ma'am; some mornings she is not well, but she is usually OK afterwards. Of course she was going to tell you herself, but I have mentioned it in view of your approving Anne and the possibility she may be able to take over."

A few days later, Adele told Amanda and asked, "May I stay on, Lady Amanda, for the time being?"

"Of course! I welcome this, but please do not strain yourself. Gerald will have told you about Anne coming to help you whilst Mr and Mrs Dansie's children are here."

"Yes, ma'am. She is a lovely girl. I know her, of course, as we live in the same village."

Nicola sent a fax listing the children's food likes and dislikes. They were beginning to realise what having three extra children for a week entailed.

Nicola asked if their young au pair should come with them. Susan said, "We will be OK on our own. Let Hope have a holiday."

They all loved her, but they wanted to be independent whilst they had the opportunity.

Nicola laughingly asked them if she might be allowed to come for the day on Wednesday. They and Amanda welcomed this. If the children hadn't settled by then, she would take them home.

Amanda prepared the menus with Gerald and Nigel. The grapevine had flourished, as had their fruit trees.

Amanda and Nicola loved each other as sisters. They were the same age. Nicola was glamorous, having been a top fashion model, and she would have liked to see Amanda wearing more 'with it' clothes, but Amanda was Amanda. She always wore well-fitted clothes and she always looked lovely, taking care of her figure and keeping her complexion and hair in tip-top condition. Nicola knew this because she often bought presents of moisturisers and shampoos/conditioners for her.

When Amanda's wedding day had been drawing near, Joan had asked her in confidence if she could come up to have a 'girlie' talk with Amanda. Nicola had the day off from her magazine. She and her au pair had taken the children to school, and then Nicola came up on the express train. She and Amanda had sat down by the river and Nicola had encouraged Amanda to talk with her.

Amanda told her about her anxieties. She was anxious about her damaged leg, which at the time had only limited flexibility. This caused Amanda concern, and she wondered how she and Mark would be able to make love.

They both had a good laugh as Nicola described positions, and Amanda began to feel more secure. Nicola stayed for lunch and then caught her train home to meet her children. When Mark had asked Joan why Nicola had visited, Joan had told him that Amanda needed a girlie talk with her.

Amanda remembered how Mark asked her to sit with him by the river. He had told her he would never do anything to hurt her. Amanda remembered also how she had cried and told him she had been concerned about her damaged leg, but he had assured her they would find their own ways. He said he would be happy just to hold her and he was so thankful she was marrying him.

She had asked, "Will we have to have our children by artificial insemination?"

She recalled how they had laughed and tension had left them.

Waves of love flowed through her as she remembered. Mark had gathered her into his shoulder with his arm round her waist and they had stayed like that, silently enjoying being one in mind and spirit.

Mark then had asked her how her dress was progressing.

She laughed now: they *had* found their own ways. She had promised Mark she would always tell him if she had any fears. He had advised her to always also ask Nicola for advice. He had then told her he had asked Joshua's advice about certain things. No wonder the four of them had a special close friendship!

Chapter 12

Every morning the five-year-old class were asked to share something special that they had achieved or wanted to share.

Heather told them, "I am designing and making my Christmas cards."

Sophie then put her hand up.

"Yes, Sophie?"

"Eric and I have bought a new camera each, to photograph unusual plants and leaves in our wood. Uncle Adam says Eric and I aren't artistic, but we can take photographs and stick them in a book and write about them."

Miss Bargh thanked the three of them. "What a good idea – capturing memories of holidays and the summer!"

Miss Bargh mentioned this to her colleagues at lunchtime. They seized on this. "Why not have a school competition designing a Christmas card?" one of them suggested. All the teachers agreed on this.

When the classes congregated together, Mrs Vine told them, "The Young children are drawing and photographing plants and leaves to make Christmas cards. In your art classes you will have the opportunity to make a card and enter a competition for the three best. You will all be winners by your achievements. Please bring card, crayons, pens, glue and anything you want to stick on your card. You will be able to keep your card afterwards."

All the children asked their parents if they could have a camera like the Young children? All the parents agreed.

Heather told Adam, who said, "What a good idea! I couldn't use these, but I will ask Ryman's if they are interested in publishing any of the best designs. If so, the money can then be used for school funds. First we must ask for Mrs Vine's approval."

Adam sent a letter with Vincent and Holly.

When Mrs Vine shared this with the teachers they were thrilled by the idea. She wrote to Adam thanking him for the thought and she said she looked forward to the project's coming into fruition. Ryman's welcomed the idea. Adam let Mrs Vine know – and also Mr Grocutt, the head of another local school. All the classes began this project.

Adam was invited to the schools to view the finished cards and choose the best three. He asked about his nephew's and nieces' work? If he chose theirs it might look like favouritism. After Mark and Amanda had spoken to the children, they understood it was awkward for Uncle Adam to choose their cards, so they put a little mark on them.

Adam was very impressed by the cards. He carefully chose the three winners from both schools. All the cards were photographed and displayed in the local library and the school hall. Adam was thinking he might have potential art designers for his unit. Perhaps Heather would be one of them! He laughed to himself.

After a few weeks Ryman's contacted him. They were using most of the cards and each had an inscription, acknowledging the individual pupil and the school. A cheque for £200 was enclosed with a letter saying that they would be interested in the school designing Easter cards.

Everyone at Chiverton was delighted. Adam took the cheque to Mrs Vine and gave her the news about the request from Ryman's for Easter-card designs.

The public-school head teacher contacted Adam. They had also had cards accepted and they too had been asked for designs for Easter. He had received a cheque for £250 as his school, having more pupils, had sent more cards. Mr Grocutt thanked Adam very much for helping them.

All this news was published in the local papers and colour magazines. The local television networks arranged to film the displays in both schools.

Mrs Vine met with the school governors to decide what they should do with the £200. After much discussion it was decided to offer it to a respite home for adults with learning disabilities.

Then Adam suggested to Mrs Vine and Mr Grocutt that all the cards be displayed in the local community hall.

This was accepted with joy. The Women's Institute set up refreshments for people to buy, and the proceeds were divided between the two schools.

The twins and triplets took beautiful photographs of leaves with rain droplets on and flowers, birds and animals. Adam was able to illustrate from these. He was looking forward to what they would photograph at Christmas. Vincent had captured a field mouse on a twig. Eric had a photograph of a most gorgeous butterfly with wings open. The adults had never seen a butterfly like it. They discovered that it was a very unusual one. Heather loved these photographs and asked her Uncle Adam if they could be transferred to small beakers to give as surprise presents to Vincent and Eric. Adam made enquiries and this was arranged.

Julian and Sandra continued to wait on the table. Julian personally attended to Mark's clothes. He kept these immaculate as Amanda expected. Sandra attended to Amanda's. They cleaned Amanda and Mark's rooms. Joan washed all the knitted and crocheted garments she had produced. Sandra had Saturdays off, Julian Sundays. She and Julian started work at 7 a.m. and finished at 2 after lunching. They were both willing to come when needed. Julian worked on Saturday mornings cleaning Amanda and Mark's rooms. Stan fed the dogs and kept them clean.

It was a happy household. Mrs Burton was past retirement age, but Joan advised Amanda to keep her on. This suited Amanda very much.

Chapter 13

Amanda and Mark had discussed Luca being their last child. At birth he was over 4½ kilos, and Gary had reassured them that Amanda's womb was very healthy.

When Luca was four months old, Amanda started dropping hints about the possibility of having another baby. The twins and triplets were such good friends, being close in age; Luca was five years younger, so he would grow up by himself. He would be lonely.

Mark laughed to himself. 'I had better not have the snip yet!' he thought.

Amanda and Mark adored their children, not because they were intelligent and musical but because they were their children. They had fun together. They were always laughing and singing, inside and out, in the grounds and wood. They loved to hear their parents playing their pianos and singing. Vincent, who grew more and more like his father, was learning the violin; it was his choice. His grandfather, Jonathan, was thrilled about this. Eric was an exceptional singer; he had lessons to train his voice.

During breakfast Vincent said, "Mum, Dad, whilst we are all together, my brother, sisters and I would like to stay and have lunch at school."

Amanda swallowed.

"We would like to spend more time with our friends. We couldn't invite them all here at teatime because we love to be with you, Mum. You are such fun. Perhaps we will be able to swim a little longer. Luca is happy in his pram."

Amanda was nearly crying. "Thank you very much," she said. "Of course stay at school if you prefer. What about food?"

"Sandwiches, fruit and a drink, Mum, please," Holly told her.

"Will you be staying at school today?"

"No, from next Monday will be OK, so we can get our lunch boxes organised. We will be able to do some homework there, and I will be able to have a game of cricket or football," Eric said. "Also, Mum, when Luca is older we will be able to play with him and take him out in his pram at teatime."

"He'll love that, thank you."

Eric was sports mad. He was taller and more sturdily built than Vincent; he looked like a rugby player. People thought he was the elder.

Mark was thinking, 'They have conspired this between them and presented their case well. Whatever will they be like in ten years?'

Stan suggested, "If you choose your lunch boxes online, I could collect them and drinks bottles from Chesterton."

They all thanked him.

"We will be able to paint something on them, Granddad," Heather suggested. "Also, Mum, Dad, we would like to come home on the school bus. It will bring us to the gate. We will have to pay. If Granddad will continue to take us, please, this would help us."

Stan looked at Amanda and Mark. They nodded.

"Of course I will, with pleasure," Stan said.

They continued eating. Amanda smiled at Mark. He understood. They knew the children had to move on.

"Also, Mum, Dad, now we are in the older class, Holly and me, if you agree, may we have music lessons – violin for me and piano for Holly?" asked Vincent.

Amanda looked at Mark, and he nodded.

"Yes, we agree to this," she said.

"OK, Mum, we will get this set up."

"Aunt Muriel is so pleased that you are all learning the piano. Is it all right for me and Aunt Muriel to continue our Wednesday afternoon lessons?"

"Yes please, Mum," Holly answered.

Eight years before, Mark had been told of a local man, Albert, who lost his right arm and whose face and neck had been badly scarred in an explosion in Afghanistan. Through this trauma he suffered shattered nerves, and this badly affected his wife and his two young sons. The boys began to be destructive at home and school. This family were Amanda and Mark's tenants. Mark suggested to Amanda that they employ Albert as a gatekeeper so people wouldn't wander into the grounds and get injured by the dogs. He worked mornings Monday to Saturday and, gradually, with support from Amanda and Mark, their lives returned to normal, for which Albert and his wife were very grateful. Mark bought him a small greenhouse with automatic windows and had it installed against the caravan. He grew vegetables from seed in the greenhouse and his family helped him to transplant them on to their allotment. After three years he had been employed full-time. In the afternoons he watched television or did crosswords.

When Mark told him about the children coming home in the school bus he said, "Please tell Lady Amanda they will be fine. I will be looking out for them – discreetly, of course!"

Mark laughed and thanked him. "Naturally Lady Amanda will be anxious for a while. The triplets are only five years old, but we have to let them be independent."

"Yes, sir, they're safe enough here."

Mrs Vine sent Mark and Amanda a letter assuring them that the triplets would stay with their classmates and one of the supervisors until Vincent and Holly fetched them. 'All the children are escorted on the buses and the driver will come up to your gate,' she wrote. 'I understand Vincent is discussing the fares with you and that you will pay weekly. Please be assured that the triplets will, like all our children, receive the greatest care.'

Mark said, "What a lovely understanding letter!"

Amanda replied, thanking Mrs Vine and confirming that Vincent was dealing with the bus fares.

Amanda was waiting outside for the children coming home. The dogs went bounding off to the gate, barking excitedly. The little bus came in view. Amanda stayed sitting, cuddling Luca. They ran up to her and, after kissing her and Luca, "It has been great, Mum," they assured her. They then ran off to change their clothes ready to have their haircuts.

Amanda laughed to herself. She said to Luca, "Oh well, darling, at least I will have you for a few years."

She had been busy, and Clove had, as usual on Monday afternoons, cut and conditioned her hair, but it had been a long day. However, she knew she would get used to it. Mark had pulled all the stops out to get home to lunch with her. Joan, Stan and Bob had been for a walk with the dogs then lunched at the Devonshire whilst she and Mark ate on their own.

Chapter 14

Joan asked Amanda, "With Sarah not coming, would you like to go into Brookwell with me? I need some buttons and a few other things."

"No, thank you, darling. I feel a little tired this morning so I will rest here with Luca."

Joan had thought Amanda looked pale during breakfast, but she knew it was her menstrual-cycle time. "OK, darling, you do that," she said. "I'll just call and get the buttons I need; then I'll come straight back. Are you comfortable?"

"Yes, thank you, Joan. I haven't begun my period yet."

Mrs Burton brought her morning glass of beer and left her. Amanda gazed at the beautiful blue sky and marvelled at the glorious scenery. She gave thanks to God, then found herself weeping that Andrew, the Contessa, her team and Sparky had not lived to see this beauty. She began to think that everyone bereaved must feel the same as she did.

When Joan returned she realised that Amanda had been crying. She sat down.

"I think you may be slightly anaemic, darling," she said. "Luca is a demanding big baby to feed. He will be able to start solids soon."

"I have so much milk, Joan. I love feeding him, as I did the other children." Amanda told Joan of her sorrow for the ones who had died.

"Paradise will be much more beautiful than this," Joan gently reminded her.

Amanda cried again.

Joan texted Mrs Burton for a glass of Lord Dansie's best-quality red wine for Lady Amanda, and then she rang Amanda's personal doctor, Gary, asking the receptionist if he could come and see Amanda that day.

Mrs Burton rushed up, with Julian carrying a tray. Julian left them.

"Are you overdoing it, milady?" she asked worriedly.

"No, Mrs Burton, I am feeling a little tired this morning – the time of the month – and I am missing the children coming home for lunch."

"Let me know if there is anything I can do, ma'am."

Amanda warmly thanked her.

"Gerald has made watercress soup for lunch. Shall I ask him to cook you some liver?"

"Yes, please, Mrs Burton." She sipped the wine, feeling strength coming back into her body. "What would I do without you, Joan?" she said.

"I'm not going anywhere, darling. I am too happy with you all."

"What about Barrie?"

"He is a friend, like Stan and Bob, that is all. I am too set in my ways to change."

Crystal fetched Luca to change him. Every morning she and Adele washed and ironed the clothes of Luca and the other children. The doctor's receptionist rang back: Gary would call on his way home for lunch.

When he arrived, he looked at Amanda. "You are pale, Lady Amanda," he said. He took a blood sample. "You are probably anaemic; this is common with young mothers."

"Why wasn't I like this after the twins and triplets?"

"You were younger. Eat plenty of spinach, watercress and liver, and keep up with the Guinness."

They exchanged pleasantries and he rushed off. Joan went upstairs with her and helped her shower and change. Then they met up with Stan and Bob for lunch and told them about the blood tests.

"Does Mark know?" Stan asked.

"No, darling, not yet. It's not necessary to tell him whilst he is working."

After lunch Amanda fed Luca; then she and Joan sat outside

again, listening to a music tape and sipping their Guinness. Joan was happily crocheting. Amanda slept. The dogs went racing down to the gate.

"Here they come!" Joan said unnecessarily.

Amanda stood up, and they ran up to her and cuddled and kissed her and Joan, telling them they had had a brilliant day.

Adele brought their fruit drinks.

"I'm not swimming today, darlings," Amanda said.

"That's OK, Mum. Have you a meeting?" Vincent asked.

"No, darling, I am spending time with you all. Would you like to ride your bicycles?"

They approved of this.

"We swam with Dad this morning." (They swam with Mark, Luke and Adam every day at about 6 a.m.)

They went with Adele to change their clothes while Joan fetched Amanda's chair. They set off on their bikes, singing at the top of their voices. The dogs were chasing about all over the place and barking; Joan and Amanda were laughing. Luca just slept through it.

When Mark came home, Amanda was upstairs with Joan. She told him about the blood tests and that the doctor had said it was usual for young mothers to be anaemic. He looked worried.

Joan reassured him: "She will be fine with eating extra iron, but if necessary she can have a course of iron pills."

Amanda had fed Luca so they went to spend time with their children before they slept.

Towards the end of the evening meal, after discussing the children's lunching at school and coming home on the bus, Luke said, "It's good that they are being independent."

Amanda started crying.

They all froze, then Mark got up and cuddled her.

"I'm so sorry I've upset you, Amanda," Luke anxiously told her. "I wouldn't hurt you for the world."

Amanda was trying to reassure him whilst still crying.

Joan spoke in her 'nanny' voice: "Amanda is in her menstrual cycle and she is also very possibly slightly anaemic. Gary has been today and he has taken a blood sample. It's not uncommon for young mothers to have anaemia, and a course of iron pills, if necessary, will help."

Amanda had quietened down. Mark had brought his chair up and was still cuddling her.

Uncle Bob quietly said, "It's opened my eyes, Amanda. I was still seeing you as a Met commander, used to dealing with hardened criminals, bravely coping with your leg, running Chiverton and everything."

They all agreed with Bob.

"Yes, this is how I see you, Amanda. I'm very pleased you are being honest with us and haven't rushed away. You have recently given birth to Luca and you feed him. He is a big baby," Luke told her.

Amanda thanked them and apologised.

They smiled at her.

"Please don't say I am nearly thirty-six years old," she joked.

Mark said, "I am nearly forty-two!"

"Keep eating the spinach," she teased. "I have to eat more spinach, watercress and liver."

"I have some barley wine that might do you good, Amanda. I was keeping it for three years, until it is fully matured, but it is near enough ready."

Joan asked him, "Please give me the ingredients and I'll ask Gary if Amanda can have it with the pills. Come on, darling – an early night!"

Amanda said "goodnight' and kissed them. She, Mark and Joan went up and Joan helped her shower.

The others stayed where they were for a while, questioning how they could help her and what they could do to cheer her up.

Luke suggested, "I'll look online for any latest release of her favourite detective DVDs or books."

They approved this and agreed to share the cost.

Mark got one of Amanda's favourite detective tapes out, had a ten-minute workout then a quick shower. Amanda was sat up in bed. Mark set up the video. Joan brought their flask of hot, milky barley cup and left them with the words "You know where I am."

They thanked her and, after kissing them, she left. Amanda patted the bed, Mark got in, put his arm round her, and told her how much he adored her and how proud he was of her for all she did and for giving birth to six beautiful children. "Don't fret about being thirty-six years old, sweetheart. You are gorgeous. Your hair, your face, your figure, your personality and – goodness, everything about you is wonderful!"

Amanda discerned that he was worried, though he did his best not to show it. "There is nothing to worry about, my darling," she said. "It's only a slight shortage of iron in my blood. With the extra iron, and possibly a course of pills, I will soon be back to full health, I promise."

He began to feel more positive, as he always did after she reassured him. She snuggled up to him and they watched the video until Brenda brought Luca. Mark and Joan asked her to have breakfast in bed.

"Thank you, darlings, I am fine," said Amanda. "I want to be up with the children before they go off."

Gary gave the all-clear for the barley wine. "Excellent!" he said. "Do you think I could have a couple of bottles? Luca will be walking at six months with this."

The next day he brought the results of the blood tests. They showed slight anaemia; otherwise everything else was healthy. Her cholesterol level was normal. He left her a course of the iron pills. He reminded her again that she was in very good health for a thirty-six-year-old.

"Next year I will be thirty-seven. Will I be too old to have another baby?"

"We'll consider that when you are ready. There should be no problem. Keep eating the spinach," he teased her. (He knew she wasn't keen on it.) "Luca's nappies will need an extra boil," he laughed.

"Uncle Bob, thank you for the barley wine. It certainly has a kick. I felt it go right through my system."

"I have more and we will continue making plenty of it to give it a chance to mature fully."

The other adults all enjoyed a glass.

Bob had come to live in the bungalow when his sister and her husband had retired to Cornwall. As it had a cellar, he began with

Stan to make beer, including lager. This was drunk at Chiverton. The barley wine was ready in twelve months, but to mature fully it really needed to be kept for three years. They had made more of this each year.

They went early to bed the next evening. Amanda told Mark, "I feel embarrassed Joan helping me shower now."

"Let her help you, darling, for a few days. She knows when not to intrude."

"You are right, sweetheart, she does. She has always been a treasure."

Next morning, whilst they were all breakfasting together, Vincent unexpectedly said to Amanda, "Mum, you are so beautiful. We are all proud of you. All our friends are jealous."

Holly then echoed him: "Yes, Mum, you are."

Amanda was dumbstruck. Then she asked jokingly, "Have I missed anything? Are you going to ask me a big favour?"

Everyone laughed.

"No, Mum, we mean it," Holly replied firmly.

The triplets then told her, "Yes, Mummy, you are beautiful."

Amanda graciously thanked them: "My wonderful children, you are beautiful, thank you." She was amazed at what they had said. All the grown-ups were.

"I always have the same hairstyle – this is easy for swimming. Please tell me if and when you are fed up with it."

"It's OK, Mum," Vincent told her.

Amanda then gave one of her sayings: "That's all right, then." They all laughed.

Amanda thanked him and then teased them: "Are you going to spring any more surprises on me?"

Mark also teased them: "Will you give us a bit more notice when you all decide to leave home, please?"

They all laughed.

"You are looking good, Amanda," Luke then told her.

She knew Luke meant she was getting her slim figure back with the swimming and exercising. She smiled at him. "I may be a little anaemic, but this is being corrected," she said.

Vincent broke in: "We didn't know that, Mum. Are you short of folic acid and vitamin B12?"

"Yes, darling."

"We studied this. You need plenty of dark-green vegetables, pulses and apricots."

"Also, Mum," Holly said, "bananas, melon, wholegrain cereals, including wholewheat, and carrots, Mum."

Amanda and the family were thrilled at the children's knowledge. Amanda was thinking, 'We are having an adult conversation!'

Mark had also picked this up and was thinking the same.

"Carrots?" queried Stan. "I thought carrots helped you see in the dark."

They all laughed good-humouredly.

"Yes, Granddad," Vincent agreed, "they do, and they also strengthen the immune system. May we ask Mr Frost for a full list?"

"Yes please. Don't tell him about me, will you?"

"Not if you don't want us to, Mum." Sophie said. "I won't tell, Mum."

Everybody laughed because they knew she probably would. She did, and word spread.

Amanda received cards, letters and flowers from well-wishers hoping she would soon be back to full health. The leaders of local churches promised to pray for her. The local papers kept the public informed about her health and said that it was a common complaint among young breastfeeding mothers. Lady Amanda was put on a course of iron pills from the doctor and she ate plenty of spinach and other sources of folic acid and vitamin B12.

"It is no bad thing, Amanda, people knowing," Mark told her. "It will reassure other young mothers; if it has happened to you with your good diet, it can happen to anyone."

Joan agreed.

Health shops sent bottles of an iron supplement. Joan called in and thanked them. She resolved to ask the doctor if Lady Amanda could have this when she had finished the pills he had prescribed.

A week later during dinner, Amanda shared with the family: "I am feeling so much stronger now. Thank you for everything." She was able to walk and swim longer.

She, Joan and Mrs Burton went into Brookwell; whilst they were in the arts-and-crafts shop she walked, pushing Luca's pram. Everyone stopped her, asked how she was and admired Luca. They were all very happy to see her.

Mark was informed by the Deputy Chief Constable that he had passed Amanda in Brookwell and that she had looked very becoming wheeling Luca. "She is walking much better now, sir."

Mark thanked him and confirmed that she was coming back to full health and strength.

Mark had never stopped thanking God for this. He had been very worried about Amanda. Knowing this, Gary had rung him to confirm that the blood tests showed she was very healthy apart from just the slight anaemia.

"Lady Amanda will follow my guidelines and there will be improvement in less than a month," Gary said.

The head gardener (Nigel) and Gerald met with Amanda on Monday mornings to discuss the vegetables and fruits that would be available for the week. After Nigel left, Gerald and Amanda prepared the menus, co-ordinating the meat and fish. Then Amanda and Mrs Burton discussed other household matters.

"The washing machines are wearing out, ma'am; we also need an extra one now."

Amanda laughed. "Three washing machines? Yes, we all must make a lot of work, and now there are the children's sports and riding clothes. May I leave this with you, Mrs Burton?"

"Of course, ma'am. Julian will be happy to arrange this. The dry-cleaning machine is still working well."

Only Julian and Sandra were allowed to use this well-ventilated machine. It was most satisfactory, especially for Mark's suits.

"We could also do with another pair of hands in the mornings. There are plenty willing to work here, Lady Amanda."

"Good. May I also leave this with you, Mrs Burton? You know the local families."

"Certainly, ma'am. I have a list of people I can call on."

Mrs Burton was always encouraged by the trust Amanda had in her. When they had finished the housekeeping business, they had their pot of tea.

"How are you, Mrs Burton?"

"I am very well, ma'am. I should be with all the good meals and fruit!" She laughed. "I would like to talk to you sometime about what you think about my beginning to train Sandra to take over from me – not for a few years yet," she hastened to add.

"Surely Sandra will marry?"

"As you know, ma'am, Julian and Sandra are good friends but, with Julian not able to have children, he thinks it unfair for Sandra to marry him."

"Yes, I appreciate that."

"But, ma'am, I believe they will marry and stay on."

"If I can help them . . ." Amanda suggested.

"They know that they can always count on your support, ma'am, but just now they are taking each day as it comes and being happy."

"I am pleased; I am very grateful to you for staying on. If there is anything I can do to lessen your load, please tell me."

"I will, Lady Amanda. All your staff know you always listen."

Amanda got up and hugged her. "You are very precious to all of us, Mrs Burton."

"Thank you, ma'am. You and your family are very precious to me. I'll go and tell Julian about getting the new machines."

Amanda thanked her.

After this, Mr Wilson (the steward of Amanda and Mark's estate) came for his monthly discussion with Amanda to tell her the needs of the tenants. Stan, Bob and their pals still went round the farms collecting the monthly rents. Joan often went with them.

Chapter 15

Whilst Amanda and Mark were soaking in their bath, after Mark had massaged Amanda's leg as always, she asked him if he would like her to take him to the Morley next week for dinner.

"I certainly would, darling. Evening dress?"

"One of your new suits and bow tie, please."

She booked the table and taxi. The staff at the Morley were thrilled they were coming; they arranged a table for their privacy.

Amanda kept her new dress in Joan's room. She asked Mark if he would get ready in his father's room. He guessed she wanted to surprise him.

"Of course, darling, Dad will be only too pleased to help," he replied.

The beautician came that morning to wax Amanda's legs and give her a manicure. Clove came to condition and style her hair. As usual, on Monday afternoons he cut all the family's hair. Sandra stayed late to give Amanda a light make-up. Before putting on her dress, Amanda gave Luca a 'top-up'.

When Amanda was ready, Joan and Sandra told her how beautiful she looked. Nicola had sent her a present of a latest-design small handbag to match the dress. Teresa had sent her a pair of sandals.

Sandra gave Amanda another coat of mascara, and before she left she told Mark that Amanda was ready to go.

He ran upstairs and when he saw her he was overwhelmed! This was the first 'floaty' dress he had seen her in – in fact, it was also a first for Amanda.

"Darling, you take my breath away," he said. "You are gorgeous!

How can you be the mother of six children?" He carefully gathered her into his arms; he was trembling.

"You look devastating, my precious husband," she murmured, kissing him.

He pulled a box out of his jacket pocket. She opened it. It was a most beautiful necklace of pale iridescent pearls. She loved it. She took off her chain and he fastened the new necklace on. It blended with her dress perfectly.

"How did you know, sweetheart?" she said.

"I had it made to match your sweet-pea material. I thought you would be wearing one of those."

"They haven't been made yet, darling, but the necklace is just perfect for this dress." She kissed him passionately.

"Watch your make-up!" he laughed.

"You are more important than make-up," she replied.

He asked, "We will not be able to stay out too late, will we? Luca will want his supper."

She laughed and promised, "No, we will get back early, darling. We had better go."

They went down in the lift. The taxi was waiting.

Stan, Bob, Luke, Adam and Joan were outside. They all told her how beautiful she looked.

She laughed. "Doesn't my husband look distinguished?"

They all agreed.

Luke, after asking permission, began to take photographs.

They walked with their arms around each other. Mark carefully handed her into the car, tucking her dress in.

During the meal Mark cherished her. They had agreed before marrying that to avoid embarrassing them they wouldn't be demonstrative in front of the family; they knew they were deeply in love and that was all that mattered. It was a wonderful evening.

Mark said, "We must do this more often."

Eventually the waiter announced that the taxi had arrived. Amanda discreetly paid with her card. They thanked the staff and said how much they had enjoyed the meal. They promised to come again soon.

After returning home, they went up to their room and Brenda

brought Luca. Whilst Amanda took her dress off and cleansed her face, Mark cuddled him and told him what a beautiful mother he had.

After Amanda had fed Luca and cuddled him, Brenda fetched him and left Mark and Amanda alone.

At breakfast Luke showed the photographs. The children were thrilled with these.

"You look different," Holly told her. "Please, Mummy, will you wear your dress for us?"

"Of course I will, my darlings."

Stan suggested they would perhaps like to have dinner on their own, but Amanda was horrified. "No, no, Dad! We treasure sharing meals with you all. Mark and I have plenty of time on our own." She laughed. "I will be taking him out again, though."

They all laughed, very relieved.

The children took the photographs of their parents to show their teachers and their friends. Luke had ten photographs enlarged and framed for the family. Mark chose one of Amanda by herself for his desk at the station, and for the side of his bed he chose one where Luke had captured her face lit up with her most beautiful smile. Teresa and Nicola were thrilled at Amanda's new look. Teresa congratulated Nicola and thanked her for this help.

"We have a glut of eggs. We can't let the local shops have them as it would be unfair to the local suppliers," Amanda shared with Sarah one day.

Sarah laughed. "The other day when I went to the farm shop they had sold out again, and it was only just after 11. Each year they get more and more visitors. Also, most mornings there is a queue of locals waiting for the shop to open. Richard is meeting with the Duke tomorrow; would you like him to mention your surplus eggs?"

"Yes, please," laughed Amanda. "We are getting overwhelmed with lemon curd."

"Have you thought of opening a farm shop, Amanda? You could sell your meats and vegetables in it."

"No, darling: (a) it would be too much commitment for us and (b) with Chatsworth being so near, it would be unfair. Also supplying Mum and Nicola, and everyone here having a good appetite, we usually do not have much to spare. All the outside staff buy eggs, etcetera at a reduced price. Also, Gerald has vegetables frozen."

"You have a good system going, darling." Sarah approved. She learned so much from Amanda.

The Duchess texted Amanda, asking, 'Please supply the shop, darling. You will get the full price less 10%. Ring me when it is convenient.'

Amanda rang and thanked her. "Do they have to be inspected, ma'am?" she asked.

"Yes, the inspectors come regularly; there will be no problem with your eggs. We will have your boxes printed out."

"I will ask Adam and Heather to make up a design."

"Also, Amanda, any time you have chickens to sell, please let me know."

"I will, but we eat such a lot of chicken."

"Another need we have, Amanda darling, is for fresh rabbits. I think our rabbits have moved to Chiverton!" She laughed.

"Rabbits are Mr Shulot's department – I will certainly ask him."

"When are you having another kite-flying afternoon, Amanda?"

"I will ask Mark, ma'am."

"We are going to the Duke's family again for a month in two weeks' time," the Duchess said. She then asked about the children. She rang off after Amanda had promised to see about arranging for a kite-flying afternoon.

Mr Shulot was delighted with the prospect of supplying the Duchess with rabbits.

Amanda told him, "All the money will be yours, less 10% for the farm shop; they will pay you. The rabbits, of course, will have to have regular inspections."

"No problem there, ma'am! No one has been poisoned yet."

They both laughed.

Bob promised he would deliver the eggs each morning after breakfast. He still had the majority of his meals with them. For the past eight years he had been treated as part of their family and he and they were grateful for this.

Chapter 16

"Do you think you could manage the open-air united service on Sunday, darling?" Mark asked Amanda. "I have been asked to read the Gospel."

"Yes, precious, as it doesn't start until 11."

Amanda wore her lavender sweat-pea long-sleeved dress with a matching wide-brimmed hat. They all told her she looked beautiful.

The leader was introduced. He was the new minister of St Peter's Methodist Church, Jon Stewart, aged thirty-four, married but with no children as yet. He encouraged all the children to take part in the service. He was a natural preacher with a good sense of humour. During the service he thanked the local dignitaries and everyone for coming, and then he announced, "We also have the honour of our new Chief Constable and his family being here. The Chief Constable will read the Gospel and his children will sing for us."

Everybody clapped and cheered. Mark stood up to acknowledge them and led the children to the stage, where they stood holding hands whilst he read the Gospel passage. Then he accompanied them as they sang.

Everyone clapped them.

Before they left the stage, Mr Stewart asked the children if they loved Jesus. They all said they did, and prayed to him.

Sophie told him, "Every day we study our weekly Bible readings."

This took him by surprise. "Do your mummy and daddy help?" he asked.

"Yes," Vincent answered, "and we have storybooks. Mum, and

Dad if he is free, reads to us every night and then before we go to sleep we pray and thank God for helping us."

"That is wonderful. What is your name, please?"

"Vincent."

The minister asked the other children's names. "Whilst you are here, may we pray for all children who do not know Jesus?"

They all nodded and put their hands together whilst he prayed. Mark and Amanda were nearly weeping.

After the service, Mark, Amanda and family mingled with the other churchgoers. Then Mr Stewart came up to Mark and Amanda and shook hands. They thanked him for the service and told him how much they had enjoyed it.

"Are you on your own?" Amanda asked him.

"No, my wife is in the worship group."

His wife then joined them.

"Are you settling here?" Amanda asked her.

"Yes, thank you, ma'am. It's a bigger community than we are used to, but everyone is making us feel welcome."

The twins and triplets came with Joan and the rest of the family. They knew Amanda couldn't stay long. They all introduced themselves.

The couple looked a little lost, so Amanda asked, "Are you busy?"

"Not now, Lady Amanda. The team are moving the chairs."

Mark nodded. He knew what was coming.

"Do you want to come back with us for lunch?"

"Oh, yes please, ma'am!" they both replied.

"Right, have you a car?"

"Yes, it is at home. I will fetch it."

Mark laughed. "No need! Our friend Mrs Hewer is here."

Muriel was coming back with them, as she did most Sundays. Now she was part of the family.

The family changed into their casuals whilst Muriel showed Jon and Sheila the changing rooms. Sandra brought them a jug of fresh lemonade.

During lunch they discovered Jon had a wonderful sense of humour. They all liked him.

112

Sheila, his wife, was shy, but Muriel sensitively drew her out. They drank spring water with the meal.

It began to pour with rain. Jon thanked God it had kept fine for the morning. They went into the sitting room for coffee and fruit juice. Mark went upstairs with Amanda to attend to Luca.

When they came down the others were all watching showjumping. All the top riders were competing. The guests stood up when Amanda came into the room.

"Please sit down. Are you all comfortable?"

They all assured her they were.

"Would you like a glass of wine, beer or Guinness?"

Jon and Sheila replied, "Guinness, please."

Amanda and the other adults had the same. They settled to watching the television. The twins and triplets were engrossed. One of the top riders knocked a pole off. The family went quiet. Then the next competitor knocked a brick off a wall, followed by the next horse refusing to go down a slope.

Amanda said, "This is bad. These horses cost thousands of pounds, and their riders rely on the winnings."

Jon was biting his tongue. He wanted to say "Oops!" whenever the poles and bricks were knocked off, but he daren't because the family were viewing so seriously.

The sun came out.

Mark asked, "Would you like to have a walk?"

They all agreed and went with the dogs. Amanda was in her chair, and Mark wheeled Luca.

When they reached the wood, Jon asked, "May I thank God for this morning's service, the sunshine and for the marvellous lunch and meeting you all?"

They all said, "Yes, please."

He gave a beautiful prayer of thanks, and then he prayed for the showjumpers and horses. He then began to sing a chorus they all knew.

They all joined in. Mark thanked him.

The dogs and children started running in the wood. The perfumes from the drying ground and trees were beautiful. They could also smell garden fires in the distance. Luke was taking photographs. They went back and had afternoon tea outside, they were all happy. Sheila had lost her shyness.

Sheila and Jon had to leave for the 6.30 service; they couldn't thank Amanda and Mark enough for the beautiful time.

Mark promised, "You will be invited again soon. We have all enjoyed your company."

The others all agreed.

"My wife will now recommence her rota of inviting local ministers and their families in turn on the first Sunday of each month. We worship at The Open Church on the remaining Sundays. I am one of the organists. The children go to Sunday school and, as Sophie told you this morning, they have Bible readings to study during the week. We will be very happy for you both to come often. We will keep in touch."

They thanked him.

"If I'm free, I will pick you up when you are coming," Muriel promised.

They thanked her.

Jon quietly asked Mark, "Sir, may I ask if anyone would like to come to our evening service?"

"Of course you may," Mark assured him.

Luke, Stan and Bob said they would. Adam said, "I can come because The Open Church is closed today. I'll ask Robert – he's the Reverend Brian's son – if he wants to join us."

Amanda asked, "What about you, Joan darling?"

"I'll stay and help with the children."

Mark told her, "If you want to go, Joan, the children will be fine with us."

She thanked him.

Luke asked, "Would you like me to bring my guitar or saxophone?"

"Saxophone, please! It will be lively worship."

"I'll bring my flute," Adam promised.

Jon thanked them. He was excited by their support.

Muriel took him and Sheila back to their home.

Chapter 17

On the first Sunday in July it was the turn for St Anne's Church. The lady vicar was still there. Her licence had been renewed. Mark happily agreed to play the piano to give Mrs Moor and Mrs Way a rest.

A new family was there. It consisted of the parents, a boy aged eight and two girls aged six and five. The children stood at the front showing the artwork they had done. Then, during the vicar's talk, the boy pulled Heather's plait hard. She winced. Holly got hold of him and threw him to the floor. Everyone went quiet. He lay there for a few seconds, then got up and said sorry to Heather. She accepted his apology. Next he held her and Holly's hands. He followed Holly about after the service. They looked the best of friends. Sophie was absolutely thrilled because the girls had brought a doll like the one she had, and they both had sparkly-trimmed tee-shirts and a book of cut-out fashion dolls.

The twins and triplets came up to Amanda with their new friends and Holly asked, "Please, Mummy, may Siobhan, Lauren and Trevor come to lunch?"

"We will need to ask their parents."

They had been talking with the Reverend Ryan. They came across and the Reverend Ryan introduced them. They were both schoolteachers.

Amanda apologised for Holly throwing Trevor.

"We thank her very much, Lady Amanda. He is getting too bossy with his school friends and his sisters. We have been trying several ways to channel his energies. We understand of course that he may be feeling insecure, with the move and settling here, but that is no excuse."

Amanda bonded with them immediately.

"Are you free to come back with us for lunch?" she said. "The children have asked."

"Yes please, ma'am. May we go home to change into more-decent clothes?"

"No, no, you are OK. It isn't the clothes but the person inside that matters. The Reverend Ryan and her family are coming also."

They were all happy.

Muriel chimed in: "Right, who is coming with me?" she asked in her forthright way.

Amanda introduced the new family.

Muriel came every Sunday she was free, and during the week she swam with Amanda. They were all great friends with Muriel. She had been a music teacher and the children practised with her. Also she had always been a Sunday-school teacher. She also did craftwork, and she was a favourite with Joan and Mrs Burton.

Luke came up laughing. "Are we ready?"

He was thinking, 'How many more are coming back with them?'

They all went into the hall. Mark was letting everyone see Luca. The children and their new friends were talking together. Trevor and Holly were still holding hands! Mr Moor then appeared and he and Mrs Moor went with Muriel. They all set off.

After arriving at Chiverton, Stan and Bob went first to control the dogs. Dennis and Yvonne were overwhelmed with Chiverton, and their children were clinging to them.

"Come on!" Vincent invited, and they all ran together up to the house.

Joan, Muriel and Stan showed Dennis and Yvonne the outdoor pool and changing rooms whilst Amanda went upstairs to feed Luca. Mark went with her. Luke and Adam served the guests freshly squeezed juice drinks. The children were running about with the golden retriever. Bob had taken Cambridge, Oxford and Thunder to the dog unit.

After Mark had said grace, they began their lunch; the children were together, the best of friends. Yvonne sat next to Amanda with her two girls at her other side. Mark was on Amanda's right, next to Graham. Mrs Ryan was next to Dennis, with Trevor on the other side of him. They conversed, getting to know one another. The twins and triplets were between Muriel, Stan, Bob, Luke and Adam for them to help them.

The new children were solidly built but not excessively so. They ate their food as though they were starving. Even Sophie ate more than usual. All the adults ate, as usual, with a good appetite.

"This food is exceptionally tasty, Lady Amanda. I have never tasted any as wonderful," Dennis remarked.

"Thank you, Mr Seddons. It is Chiverton produce. Tuck in, please, all of you. There is plenty."

Gerald, Anne and Sandra brought more dishes in.

They did tuck in as Amanda had invited. They drank spring water with the meal.

Luke told them, "It's Chiverton water. We have our own spring and the water is purified."

"Is the spring water used for the pool," Yvonne asked.

"No, the pools and toilets are supplied from the mains. Every drop of water we use is recycled for the gardens, the greenhouses and, when needed, the sprinklers for the grass. Nothing is wasted here," Mark informed them. He was secretly laughing; he thought he had better not, whilst they were eating, mention that the waste from the toilets was also recycled.

For dessert they were offered rhubarb crumble with ice cream or custard, or fresh peaches. Everyone went for the crumble and ice cream.

Mark told them, laughing, "The ice cream is also Chiverton-made. Our chef is always prepared on Sundays for extra guests."

They all laughed.

"On the first Sunday of each month we go round the churches. We all enjoy this and it is a good way of getting to know people. The ministers and their families often come back with us. It is a long-standing arrangement, apart from when I am in my first and third trimesters and then for the first six months of feeding a new baby."

"I breastfed my babies," Yvonne shyly said.

Amanda beamed at her; she knew they would become good friends.

Crystal brought Luca after making him comfortable; he was making his happy sounds. Mark lifted him out of his pram.

"Are you new to St Anne's?" Mark asked them.

"Yes, sir. I was promoted to teaching fourteen- to sixteen-year-olds. Yvonne works part-time, and she was given an opportunity, so that is why we moved from Peterborough. We miss our friends and the local church fellowship, but Reverend Ryan and everyone have made us feel welcome. The children are settling down."

"They look as though they are now," Luke laughed.

They all agreed.

Graham closed the meal with a prayer. Then they all went to stretch their legs and met at the outdoor tables for coffee or fruit drinks.

Sophie asked, "Please, Mummy, may I take Siobhan and Lauren to my room so I can show them my dolls?"

"Ask their parents, darling."

Of course they agreed.

Trevor went with the other children to see their ponies.

Later all the children came running back.

Vincent asked, "Please, Dad, may we fly our kites?"

Mark looked round and asked, "Are we up to it?"

"Yes, please."

"We promised to let the Duke and Duchess know when we were kite-flying. Is this OK with everyone?"

They agreed.

Mark texted the Duke and Lord Richard, inviting them if they were free that afternoon to come and join in the kite-flying.

They accepted with delight.

Amanda then texted Gerald, asking him to arrange afternoon tea for 5.30 and she informed him that there would be extra guests. Amanda and Mark took their children upstairs to change whilst everyone else made themselves comfortable at the outdoor-pool changing rooms and had a look around.

Mrs Moor had asked if she might stay at the table as she always did. Joan brought two CDs, the player and her knitting. Mrs Burton joined them with a twinkle in her eye.

"Shall we fetch a pot of tea?" she asked.

Anne brought the tray.

The Duke and Duchess, Lord Richard and Lady Sarah arrived with Angela in her pushchair. After introducing one another, they set off with their kites. Luke had fetched enough for the new family, the Reverend Ryan and her husband. Amanda was in her battery chair. Amanda and Mark had had the piece of field fenced off to keep the animals out. They had wooden tables and chairs put around.

They all had a wonderful afternoon; the only sadness was that the Reverend Ryan and Muriel had to leave for their evening services. The Duke had been very interested in Graham's account of the youth activities and the meeting and the midweek community meal held once a month at St Anne's Church.

The Duke promised, "My wife and I will come to one of these when we are free – low profile."

"Of course, sir."

"We will let you know."

Everyone trooped back to the house for the afternoon tea.

As the children were being rounded up, Amanda, with Mark's permission, invited the Seddons family to return next Sunday if they wished.

They certainly did, and they thanked her.

"Please come after the service," said Amanda. "I will be here. The family go to The Open Church; the children are given their daily Bible readings. It's a little far for me whilst I am feeding Luca."

Sophie asked, "Please, Mummy, Daddy, may our friends come again next Sunday?"

Amanda smiled. "They are invited, darling," she said.

The children went to the car with the Seddons. Sophie, Holly and Heather kissed the girls. Sophie stood waving until the car was out of sight. Mark went to fetch her.

"I love Siobhan and Lauren, Daddy."

"Yes, darling, they are lovely, like you are."

He sat at the table with her and she showed him the book of cut-out dolls they had left with her.

Later, when he and Amanda were having their soak in the bath, he told her, "I only realised today that, although Sophie is the best of friends with her brothers and sisters, she must also be a little lonely. The others don't really understand her love of sparklies and fashion."

"Yes," agreed Amanda, "I was thinking the same thing. God is good; He has provided her with like-minded friends now. I like the parents."

Mark said he did also.

The following Sunday, Trevor, Siobhan and Lauren told the church they were going to Chiverton Manor.

When they arrived Dennis laughingly told Mark and Amanda, "Yvonne and I have had the most marvellous week with the children. They have gone to bed and tidied their rooms without arguing."

"We did threaten that if they didn't behave, they couldn't come to visit you," Yvonne told them.

Everyone laughed. None of the children had wanted to be left out.

Yvonne and Dennis and the children along with Jon and Sheila were regular visitors to Chiverton. They all loved one another and enjoyed being together doing various activities.

Chapter 18

The Duchess texted Amanda: 'Please ring me as soon as possible, darling. I am in the office all morning.'

"Is anything wrong, ma'am?"

"No, darling, it's good news. May I pop round now?"

"Of course. I'll order a pot of tea."

When the Duchess arrived, she came straight to the point: "The Queen, Prince Philip and Princess Anne are coming overnight on Friday July 28th before going on to the races. They have asked me whether coming to you for lunch and afternoon tea will be too much for you just now."

"Oh no, ma'am. This would be wonderful."

"I knew you would say that. They are coming to congratulate Mark on his promotion, and also you and Josh for rescuing the factory. They will relax with you so I suggest an informal lunch, though you could of course invite your parents and Josh and family. I thought Richard and Sarah might come as well."

"Of course they must be invited."

"Yes, darling, that will be lovely. Would you and Mark like to come for dinner on the Friday evening? The Queen's lady-in-waiting asks for it to be a light meal at 7.30 to finish at 9.30 so the royals may have an early night before travelling the next morning. Also, Amanda, I know they have seen you often since you were shot, but you have their greatest admiration for how you have coped and continue to cope. What a wonderful Christian example you set everyone!"

"Thank you for that, ma'am."

"Keep it informal. The Queen is coming to relax with you. Would you like our butler to come to help?"

"Oh, yes please, ma'am; that would be perfect. Everyone serving will be nervous."

"Will Mark ensure discreet security is set up?"

"Yes, of course. Do you think we should also invite Divisional Commander Draycott and his wife?"

"That would be good. You invite them. I must go now, darling. Thanks for seeing me so quickly. We will keep this mum for the minute; let the community know soon, of course."

They kissed. The Duchess looked at Luca in his pram.

"I'll not disturb him," she said. "He is bigger every time I see him."

They laughed.

After the Duchess had left, Amanda sat thinking how lovely it was that the Queen was actually coming to visit them. She began to feel nervous but calmed the nerves. She resolved to do her best to make her guests feel relaxed. She knew them and they knew her. She had often been to Balmoral and other royal homes, and on many occasions she had been responsible for the Queen's security on her walkabouts. The Queen and Prince Philip had attended their wedding. 'Right,' she thought, 'Sarah isn't available today for our swim, so I'll use the time to set the wheels in motion!'

Amanda had found Balmoral too much for her damaged leg when she and Mark had gone for a few days as invited, but she had appreciated the Queen's sympathy when her beloved Contessa had died.

Luca woke up. Amanda lifted him up and cuddled him, telling him about the prospective visitors. She sat with him looking out over the grounds, thanking God for this opportunity to have the Queen relaxing at Chiverton with them. She was then filled with determination that they all would enjoy it.

She knew her mother would be at home that morning, organising a dinner she was hosting that evening. She rang her using her secure line.

"Mum, darling, how are you this morning? I am sorry to interrupt – I know you are busy – but I have a wonderful surprise for you. Charlotte has just been and she tells me the Queen, Prince Philip and Princess Anne are coming to Chatsworth on Friday July 28th before going to the horse races. They are coming here for Friday lunch. Please try to be free for this. Also, Mum, may I have Marco and his assistant again, please?"

"Of course, darling, and your dada will send the finest wines."

"Thank you, darling Mum. The Duchess's butler is also coming to help. I will let Joshua and Nicola know this evening. Enjoy your dinner, darling."

Mark had meetings again. He had to move round the stations, so he wasn't able to come home for lunch. Amanda made sure he had nourishing sandwiches and fruit. He usually worked through to ensure getting home by early evening to spend time with his children. Also, he held meetings with his colleagues in his private office at Chiverton. These were very useful when he wanted to discuss matters in privacy. His colleagues brought their own lunches to these meetings. Mrs Burton supplied them with spring water, coffee and fruit; they all knew they could ask for anything. Amanda's hospitality was first class.

Luca was happily making noises, kicking his legs and waving his arms in his pram. Amanda began to make lists. With her supports in her bathroom it wouldn't be appropriate for the Queen to use their rooms, so her parents' rooms would be the next best thing. She decided to ask her mother if they minded her having their furniture moved for the day.

Whilst she was thinking this, her mother rang back: "Darling, I have texted your dada. He will do his best to get the day off. He will send the wines as usual. If there is anything else we can help you with, let us know."

"Well, Mum, there is. I am trying to decide which rooms the Queen and the Duke will use. Mine is inappropriate because of my disability aids, but may I have your furniture moved for the day into Room 6?"

"Of course, darling. Leave us there. I am positive they will visit you often now that the Queen is handing more overseas visits to the younger royals."

"But Room 6 hasn't a balcony, Mum."

"Darling, we come to stay with you, not sit on the balcony!" She laughed. "What about armchairs?"

"Yes, we had better have three for your old room and two for Room 8 for Princess Anne."

"May I buy these for you from the store, darling?"

"If that is what you want, Mum. Let me think about the fabrics and colours."

"Let me know quickly, darling, and anything else you need whilst the van is delivering."

"I will, Mum, thank you. Don't forget the footstools!"

She texted Mrs Burton to ask if she and Gerald could possibly spare time to help her that afternoon at 2.30 before the children came home, or the next morning at 10.30.

Mrs Burton texted back: 'This afternoon, ma'am.'

Crystal fetched Luca, and Amanda went up with them. She then rang the manager of the decorators she used and made an appointment for him to come at two o'clock the next afternoon.

She laughed to Luca, "There, the wheels are in motion!"

She went down to lunch with Joan, Stan and Bob. She had to use her police training to hide her excitement. She had decided not to tell them her news until she had spoken to Mark. She went upstairs to feed Luca, and then left Crystal to make him comfortable and bring him down at three o'clock.

Gerald and Mrs Burton got their notebooks out. Amanda told them about the forthcoming visit. They were overwhelmed.

"I haven't told my husband yet, but we need to get organised for this. Marcos and his assistant will come up and the Duke's butler will oversee everything. Possibly the Morley and the Devonshire will be booked up when people know the Queen is coming."

"Yes, ma'am, I would think so," agreed Gerald.

"Which chefs and waiters would you like from the agency, Gerald?"

"May I wait until we see the menu, Lady Amanda?"

"The Queen's lady-in-waiting is faxing the suggested menu tomorrow, Gerald. This will make it easier for us."

Gerald left them.

"I will need to go round with you, Mrs Burton, to see what

needs doing. Is tomorrow morning convenient?"

"I will make sure I am available, ma'am."

"Here's Luca. Have you time for a glass of barley wine, Mrs Burton?"

"Yes please."

Mrs Burton rang the kitchen.

"Thankfully the sitting room has been decorated. The curtains and covers look lovely, don't they, Mrs Burton?"

"They do, ma'am – beautiful!"

"It is doubtful they will use the sitting room in the time they are here unless it's pouring with rain, but we will be prepared. You understand I will need everywhere to look sparkling. Please employ as much help as you need, Mrs Burton."

"I will, ma'am. There are plenty willing. I am thinking about the hall chandelier. It has been dusted, along with the ceiling and walls of course, but it hasn't been taken down and washed. I'll look in Mrs Ashby's records to see who did it the last time."

"Thank you, Mrs Burton."

Amanda lifted Luca out of his pram and cuddled him on her knee. "This is a great honour," she said. "When people get to know they will be so pleased. I can't wait to tell my husband, Mrs Burton."

"You are a wonderful lady, ma'am."

"You are used to the royals, with you helping when they came to Chatsworth, Mrs Burton."

"They haven't been for over twenty years. With Princess Diana dying, and all that has happened since, the Queen tends to stay at home as much as possible."

"Life is strange, isn't it, Mrs Burton? I have been missing the children coming home for lunch and now we have this visit to organise as well as my helping with the factory."

They both laughed.

"At least we have three weeks!"

"Good job, ma'am!" Mrs Burton laughed. "Here come the children. They look happy as always."

"I had better not tell them yet, Mrs Burton."

"Good gracious no, ma'am!" Mrs Burton greeted the children then left them.

Adele came with their fruit drinks.

"I haven't put my costume on yet. I'll meet you at the pool. Wait for me," Amanda told them sternly.

Adele was smiling. Luca was happy in his pram at the side of the pool whilst they swam and played games. Amanda showered with her girls whilst Crystal took care of Luca. Adele came and supervised the children.

Amanda fed Luca and changed into one of her new ginghams; then she went back down to join the children for their supper and waited for Mark to come home. He came running and kissed all of them; then, whilst they finished their supper, he went for a quick shower and changed into his casuals. He met them upstairs. He went with his boys for their workout and talk. Amanda listened and talked with her girls as they did on most weekdays. (On Saturdays and Sundays they all joined up.) Then they all met up for a bedtime story and prayers, and Amanda and Mark kissed all the children goodnight.

It was 7 p.m.; dinner was at 7.15.

"Just give me a minute, darling," Amanda said, and she took him into their room. "We'll talk again later, but I must tell you this before I burst: Charlotte came this morning – the Queen, Prince Philip and Princess Anne are coming here for lunch on Friday July 28th. They will spend the night at Chatsworth before leaving early for the local horse racing. They want to congratulate you on your promotion and Josh and I for helping the factory."

Mark was thrilled. "This is wonderful news for us and the whole community," he said. "We'd better go, darling – they will be getting worried."

The meal opened with a prayer as always. They tucked in.

When they had eaten, Mark said, "Amanda has some news. She has just told me."

"Sorry I didn't share this earlier, but you will appreciate I wanted Mark to know first." She told them about the visit.

They were all thrilled, and Bob said it would be a wonderful boost for the community.

"It will be a relaxed, informal meal with the Duke and Duchess, Richard, Sarah, Mum, Dada, Josh, Nicola and children. I suggested the Divisional Commander and Mrs Draycott. Is this all right, Mark?"

126

"Yes, darling, they will feel honoured to be invited. I'll let him know tomorrow. I will also need him to help me with security."

"Will you be able to have the day off, Luke and Adam?"

Luke said, "I'll take a few days' holiday. I may be able to help."

"Thank you, Luke."

Adam laughed. "I've just realised I will have to have your permission, Amanda."

"Oh well, in that case I don't think so," she teased laughingly.

"The Duke's butler is coming to oversee the waiters. He will brief everyone about the etiquette."

Stan told her, "We are very proud for you, Amanda. We will all help you prepare."

"They are coming to congratulate Mark on his promotion and thank Josh and me for taking on the factory, safeguarding jobs and increasing the local commerce. After lunch while they rest they have made a request for Mark and me to sing, then the children. I thought I would ask if Rose might be allowed to dance. They will have a walk and return here for afternoon tea. Mark and I have been invited to dinner at Chatsworth – not full dress."

"What does that mean, Amanda?" asked Adam.

"Not long evening dresses; men wearing a suit with bow tie."

Bob asked, "Should I be included in the lunch?" Joan also asked the same question.

Amanda told them sternly, "Of course you are included – you are family."

They both apologised.

"I will have a new suit made," Bob said.

Stan, Luke and Adam said laughingly that they would also.

Mark came in with, "I have mine."

"What about you, Joan? You have beautiful clothes, but do you want Jean to make you an outfit?"

"Thank you, darling. What will you wear, Amanda?"

"I thought one of my long-sleeved sweet-pea dresses would be appropriate. I'll find out what colours the Queen and Princess Anne are wearing. I have the beautiful flowered silk my Mum sent."

"I'd love a dress in that, please, Amanda."

"Ask Jean, darling. It's going to be awkward not letting on yet."

They all laughed.

"Better not tell the children!" Joan advised.

They all laughingly agreed with her.

Bob then told Amanda, "This is a great honour; we will all help you."

She thanked them.

"You will need to instruct us on the etiquette, Amanda. Mrs Burton is experienced from helping when the Queen came to Chatsworth previously."

"Yes," agreed Bob, "but she hasn't been involved with royalty for years."

"I have started a list of jobs that will need doing. Will you be free tomorrow morning, darling?" Amanda asked Joan.

"Yes."

"I would like you to come with Mrs Burton and me to look to see where we need to decorate and whatever." She told Joan, "The Queen and Prince Philip will use Mum and Dada's rooms. They will use Room 6 and Princess Anne will use Room 8. Another thing I must mention: Mark and I are invited to dinner at Chatsworth that evening at 7.30. We will be home 9.30 for the royals to have an early night before travelling early next morning to the races. Afterwards they are going on to friends in this area for the night."

"That will be lovely for you, Amanda – to go there and relax after the busy day," said Stan.

"Thank you, Dad, yes; and it will fit in with my feeding Luca. I have been missing the children coming home for lunch, and now I have this day to organise for. On top of that I am also helping with the factory."

They all laughed. They were all excited.

"I don't think I will be able to sleep tonight," Amanda said.

"You'd better have two lots of the barley-cup drink then," Joan suggested smilingly.

Amanda rang Joshua and Nicola, inviting them.

"We are so proud, darling, thank you. We will be with you. What about the children?"

"Naturally they are invited."

"We won't tell them yet!"

Amanda knew from their voices that her mother had already rung them!

The Duke's PA faxed Amanda the next day with the suggested menu and itinerary. 'The royal family will arrive at 11.45 for lunch at 12.15. After lunch, whilst the Queen and Prince Philip rest, they would like you and Mark to sing, then the children. A walk and return for afternoon tea at 4.15. Leave 5.15. Family photographs permitted.'

Amanda suggested to the Duchess that Rose dance for the royal visitors. This was welcomed, and Rose and everyone else was thrilled about it.

Mrs Burton, Joan and Amanda went round making notes of where needed decorating or cleaning. The gorgeous forty-piece bone-china dinner service and the tea-and-coffee service the Contessa had had made for them as a wedding present had lain in the cabinet, untouched but on view. Now they would be brought out. The design had been based around photographs of Chiverton which Luke had provided. It was absolutely glorious. Chiverton was shown in all its glory, full of sunshine. The lake and river gleamed, the colours of the wood and countryside were striking. Amanda and Mark had approved the design. The Contessa had requested Amanda use it, but the pieces were irreplaceable.

Mrs Burton suggested, "Nearer the time should I ask Mrs Shulot to wash it? She is so careful. I will clean all the silver."

"Thank you, Mrs Burton. I think the Queen will like the Chiverton teapots, but please prepare the silver also for the coffee."

She was very thankful she had these as well as the crystal glasses the Contessa had given her. Some of these had been used before but they were in perfect condition.

"Have I to ask Mrs Shulot to wash all of them, ma'am?"

"Yes please, Mrs Burton. I know she enjoys these jobs."

Stan and Bob offered to help Mrs Shulot transport all the glass and crockery. She always very carefully washed everything that was special in warm water without detergent.

Amanda gave Gerald the menu. Everything on it could be made from their fresh produce.

Amanda met with Nigel. "The long-range weather forecast is

good, ma'am. I suggest the lawns be mown and hedges cut on the Tuesday and Wednesday; the lane and drive could be swept on the Thursday."

Amanda suggested, "Shall I ask Mr Shulot and his sons to help with this work and the stables? They could groom the ponies early on Friday morning. Stan as usual will attend to the dogs."

Nigel welcomed this. He wrote everything down; Amanda typed into her laptop.

A buzz was in the community; they knew something important was happening. The reporters asked Amanda to let them know what was going on.

"I can't. It is not my prerogative."

The Duke, however, did give out the news of the royal visit. The local networks, papers and magazines were thrilled to announce it, and they gave the time and route the royal family would take as they travelled to Chiverton Manor for lunch. They asked Amanda if she would let them have an old photograph of herself in her commander's uniform accompanying the Queen on a walkabout as her personal security. They also asked for pictures of Amanda horse-riding with the Queen at Sandringham and having a barbecue with all the royal family.

Amanda asked the Duke's advice. He gladly gave his approval.

The Duke stressed to the media that the lunch and the whole visit would be a relaxed, informal time for the royal family. Filming and photographs along the route were allowed.

The town council contacted the Duchess, asking if they could put flower arrangements about. The local hotels and pubs were booked up and the Women's Institute planned to open the community hall to provide light refreshments. As it was the summer break the children could see the Queen passing. Everyone was so excited and proud that she was coming to their area.

Amanda asked Mr Shulot and sons, who were glad to be asked to help.

He said, "They won't need much security, milady. We will be out with our dogs!"

Amanda laughed to herself, silently agreeing with him.

Mrs Shulot promised to wash the precious china, and she asked Mrs Burton to make sure no one spoke to her whilst she was doing this and washing the crystal. She was grateful that Stan and Bob had promised to help her transport these.

The teachers asked the twins and triplets to bring photographs of the royal visit to show the other children, when they returned to school in September.

The daily routine was carried out. The factory was operating smoothly and they had received an order they had previously lost when the outdated machines were unable to meet the deadline. This and the visit of the royal family had really uplifted the whole community.

They woke to another beautiful sunny morning. Before they began their breakfast they had a time of thanking God for the beautiful sunshine. Mark, Luke and Adam swam with the children to calm them down. Amanda checked on the suites. They looked glorious. Her mother had sent a four-seater settee and three armchairs, two footstools and a large coffee table on which was an arrangement of Mark's sweet peas. The fragrance was enchanting. Other flower arrangements were around the room. Princess Anne's room was smaller, as she would be coming on her own this time. There were three new armchairs in her room, and a coffee table again with an arrangement of sweet peas. Other flower arrangements were placed around the room also.

They were all prepared for their visitors. Amanda wore her lavender long-sleeved sweet-pea dress and the iridescent pearl necklace.

The Queen and Princess Anne came in long-sleeved dresses. They wore no hats, which was customary for an informal visit. The car stopped at several points for the Queen's lady-in-waiting to receive flowers from local well-wishers and for photographs to be taken. The Salvation Army band played on the village green. The car slowed down for this. All the way the Queen, Prince Philip and Princess Anne waved and smiled. Everyone could tell they were delighted to be visiting Chiverton.

When the cars came in view at Chiverton Manor, everyone was so awed that the royal family were actually there. They were all trying not to cry with joy. Everywhere looked glorious. The sun shone from a clear blue sky, the lake gleamed and birds and insects flew and hovered overhead. The manicured grass looked perfect. The flowers and trees were full of colour. Amanda was determined that the Queen would relax and enjoy herself.

The cars stopped, and when they got out Amanda curtsied as best she could. The Queen and Princess Anne kissed her on both cheeks. They shook hands with Mark and said good morning to everyone waiting. Luke had been given permission and was discreetly photographing. Adam was filming. The Queen's lady-in-waiting had asked for the Queen to be sent copies of the film and photographs.

The royal party stood looking at Chiverton Manor and the grounds. The dogs were under control in the distance.

They went into the hall. The Queen remarked to Amanda how beautiful everywhere was. The urns of flowers were glorious; the perfume from the sweet peas filled the air; the chandelier sparkled like diamonds.

Mark, the butler and Princess Anne went up the stairs rather than waiting for the elevator. After showing their guests to their rooms, Amanda and Mark left and went back downstairs to wait in the hall. The flowers which the Queen had collected en route were put in the cold cellar.

Amanda with the Queen, and Mark with the Prince, led everyone into the dining room. As before for the celebrations, it looked spectacular. The silver and crystal glasses gleamed in the sunshine. The flower arrangements were particularly spectacular.

Mark said grace and they all tucked in. The waiters were nervous and thankful for the support of the Duke's butler. Everything went smoothly and everyone was relaxed. The Queen sat next to Amanda with Lady Teresa on her other side. Prince Philip sat between Mark and the Divisional Commander. Princess Anne was next to Adam, whom she questioned about the factory.

The butler announced, "Her Majesty the Queen will say a few words."

Everyone stood up.

"I thank Lady Amanda and the Chief Constable for the wonderful lunch and fellowship. I ask you to raise your glasses in congratulating the Chief Constable on his new position. He will,

I'm sure, make a first-class job of it. Also, congratulations and thanks to Lady Amanda and Mr Joshua Dansie for rescuing the Bryden factory, saving jobs and boosting the local economy."

They all drank then sat down.

Stan brought the meal to a close with a prayer of thankfulness.

Amanda and Mark escorted the royals to the elevator again. Amanda went to a downstairs room to feed Luca. Everyone went to the pool facilities and returned to the outside tables, where they were served coffee and the children fruit drinks. The Queen, Prince Philip, Princess Anne and the Duke and Duchess were served coffee in the Queen's room. When they had come back down they all went into the music room.

Mark and Amanda sang two of the Queen and Prince Philip's favourites. Then Amanda accompanied her father playing his violin. Mark played whilst the children sang; they were so pure and innocent. Everyone clapped them heartedly. They curtsied or bowed and then sat down. Rose came to dance. Luke set the tape going. They all enjoyed watching her; she was so professional and graceful. She received much applause. The Brookwell Male Voice Choir then sang two Scottish ballads and, to finalise, with the words displayed on a screen, they all sang one of the Queen's favourite hymns: 'O Lord My God, When I in Awesome Wonder Consider All the Works Thy Hand Has Done'. It was a very special time.

The Queen said they were ready for a walk. Prince Philip asked, "May I view the cars that are entered for the rally?"

The Queen laughingly agreed.

The Duke also asked permission.

They set off, after changing their shoes and putting sun hats on. Stan and Bob proudly escorted the Prince and the Duke. Prince Philip was interested in the wind turbines.

Stan told him it had been Mark's idea to have them installed. "Also, sir, Mark organised for all the water from the pools and everything to be recycled for the gardens, greenhouses and lawns. Waste from the toilets is recycled separately and put into the compost heaps."

Prince Philip laughed. "I must tell Prince Charles," he said. "He will want to see these operations."

"We would be very honoured to show him, sir," Stan told him as they went to see the cars.

Amanda was in her chair and Mark wheeled Luca. The dogs were running about at the Queen's request. Princess Anne was taking photographs. They reached the woods, after stopping several times to look round. The guests were all interested in the stream running down the field to the river and the watercress growing at the sides. The Queen told Amanda everywhere was so beautiful and that she was so glad they had visited.

Amanda could see Mr Shulot and his sons at various points with the dogs, as well as the discreet police security. The Queen looked as though she could walk for ever. She had taken over wheeling Luca. Luke was telling her about the kite-flying. She laughed at this. She walked with the children, asking them about school. Princess Anne also walked with the children, asking questions.

As promised, Luke sent a few relaxed photographs to the local networks, newspapers, advertisers and colour magazines.

They returned from the walk and met for afternoon tea, sitting outside under the shades. Then, it was time for them to leave. The chauffeur and butler lifted a heavy wrapped item out of the car. The Queen nodded and they took the packaging off. It was a portrait, painted from a photograph, of Amanda and Mark walking down the aisle after their marriage. It was outstanding. The artist had captured Amanda's face in all its virginal beauty and Mark brimming over with happiness. It was such an unexpected present!

Amanda and Mark, weeping, managed to thank the Queen and Prince Philip.

"We didn't want to upset you," Prince Philip quipped.

Everyone laughed.

"The artist is a young man in one of Prince Charles's youth projects," the Queen told them.

The Queen and Princes Anne kissed Amanda again and thanked her for the delightful time. They drove off while everyone waved. There were photographers waiting at the gate!

Amanda and the remaining guests sat down again and had a fresh round of drinks. Everyone was sad the royals had left. They all gazed at the portrait. The children went running about with the dogs. Everyone congratulated Amanda, who, as always, insisted it was teamwork. Her parents, Joshua, Nicola and family were taken for their train; the Divisional Commander's car came and the family were left on their own. Amanda arranged for the staff to come to be thanked. Lord Jonathan gave Mrs Burton a bonus to be shared out amongst the staff.

When Divisional Commander and Mrs Draycott arrived home they discussed what a wonderful day it had been.

"Lady Amanda was so natural and relaxed," Mrs Draycott said wistfully. "I feel I have been uptight."

"Now, poppet, as I told you this morning, this was a first for us. Imagine lunching with the Queen! You were just right."

"Thank you."

"Lady Amanda is used to royalty. She was a Metropolitan commander at a young age. She has a very high IQ, and she speaks with the same respect to everyone as she does the Queen."

"Yes," she agreed, "but that's it: I would have been boasting about Their Majesties' coming. I would have been gushing over them."

"Well, now you have seen how she behaved, you can follow her example."

"I'll try."

After discussing the day with the family and trying to decide where to hang the portrait, Amanda and Mark went upstairs with Luca. When he had been fed, Amanda and Mark prepared to be fetched to Chatsworth. The children were allowed to stay up half an hour later as it was Friday and it had been a special day. Also they wanted to see their parents in their evening clothes.

Everyone told Amanda she looked beautiful in her black embroidered voile dress and told Mark how distinguished he looked in his suit with a bow tie. The children and Luke took photographs of them in different poses. They kissed the children goodnight, told them to sleep well, and then they set off.

There were photographers waiting for them at the gate, and Amanda and Mark good-naturedly invited them in for a few minutes and got out of the car to be photographed in relaxed poses. There was one particularly special photograph where Amanda and Mark were gazing into each other's eyes. A ring of light was around them, as it had been when they took their marriage vows before God. The photograph seemed to exemplify total commitment and perfect love.

At the end of the evening when they returned home they had a few minutes outside, sharing the evening with the family. They then went upstairs to see Luca and then to bed.

The following morning Mark had to deal with calls he had received and correspondence; the children as usual groomed their ponies before riding. Amanda had promised Nigel she would come to see him in the gardens. In one of her gingham dresses and a sun hat she happily wheeled Luca while Nigel showed her the fruits and vegetables that would be ready for the preserving week.

"Everything looks healthy, Nigel."

"Yes, ma'am. We are still using the special compost, and it has been well bedded in the soil over the years. We have an advantage in having cows, goats and sheep, ma'am."

"Yes," she laughed, "and composting the peelings helps too."

She thanked the gardeners and went to sit at the outside table, where she drank a glass of barley wine and fed Luca with his fruit drink. Softly singing she cuddled him. He fell asleep. She then lifted her laptop from Luca's pram and began typing more of the Sparky story she was writing.

Joan and Mrs Burton had gone to a local fête, as they did most Saturdays during the summer. Stan and Bob had taken their sandwiches and drinks to the garage.

Two beautiful bouquets and thank-you letters had come for Amanda. One was from the Duke and Duchess and the other from the Divisional Commander and Mrs Draycott. Luke had the films developed, and they chose the ones to send to the Queen and Prince Philip. Luke also included photographs of the Bugatti.

A portrait of Contessa Sophie was over the fireplace in the sitting room. It showed her in all her beauty when she was thirty, wearing a red velvet evening dress and a diamond necklace and bracelet, with her long, curly black hair held back with a diamond tiara. Amanda had worn the jewellery for her wedding and it now belonged to her. This portrait showed a vivid likeness to Amanda.

After much discussion about where to hang the portrait the Queen had given them, they decided on the half landing facing down the first flight of stairs before they branched off to the left and the right.

Mark said, "It will be a lovely welcome as it is clearly visible from the hall as soon as you enter the house."

"For me, the entrance to Chiverton symbolises a new beginning," Amanda said quietly. "When I married you, my darling, it was the beginning of my life."

No one spoke for a few minutes.

"I suggest we commission a companion portrait of you, Mark, in your uniform, painted from one of Luke's photographs." (Mark only wore this for official occasions.) "Then another painting of us with all the children. That would symbolise continuation."

They all thought this was a brilliant idea. Bob suggested they ask a brilliant local artist.

The artist happily welcomed this commission, but she said she would also need at least two sittings for each painting.

When the news of the portrait spread, the local networks, reporters and the local monthly colour magazine asked for one of Luke's photographs. Mark and Amanda agreed.

The Queen wrote a personal letter thanking Mark and Amanda for the delightful afternoon. She said that she, Prince Philip and Princess Anne had enjoyed every minute, and that they would like to return, possibly during the third week in September, for an informal family lunch and afternoon. They would travel in a helicopter and use the helipad at Chiverton Manor. The Queen requested that rain or shine she would like to see the gardens. Prince Philip asked if it would be possible for the Bugatti to be transported to Chiverton so that he could see it.

Another letter was received from Princess Anne, thanking them and requesting, on a future visit, to see the children's ponies.

Amanda was crying with joy. She rang her mum to tell her.

Teresa laughed. "There! I told you, didn't I, darling?"

Amanda had, with Andrew's parents' permission seven years previously, sold the two-seater helicopter they had bought her and Andrew as an engagement present. The cockpit had been too cramped for her damaged leg. She had kept the helipad.

When Stan and Bob told their pals about Prince Philip's request to see the Bugatti, Barrie said, "Right, let's try to get it repaired. Wouldn't it be wonderful if he could have a ride in it?"

They searched online for the parts they needed, and eventually a garage some distance away e-mailed Barrie to say that they had traced the necessary parts. They warned that they were not cheap. They agreed to bring them to Northampton.

Barrie rang Stan and told him. "Shall we order?" he asked.

Stan suggested they go to see them first, and he contacted a coach firm which ran regular trips to Northampton. He booked seats and Barrie booked lunch at a nearby hotel. They were all excited.

Joan and Mrs Burton went with them and went shopping for presents before meeting them for lunch. The men were jubilant: they had what the Bugatti needed. The garage was going to deliver them free. They all went back to the Brookwell garage.

Stan let Mr Crosslie know about this. He was very pleased and thankful he hadn't let the car go as scrap. Amanda told Andrew's parents, who always kept in contact. Whenever they came over from Portugal they came to Chiverton. They adored the children.

Chapter 19

Vincent and Holly asked their father if they could visit Chesterton Police Station during the summer break. Mark was thrilled; they always maintained that they were going to be police officers. He arranged for all of them to go and had the day off. He had worked so much overtime.

Joan called at a local well-known store which has a baby feeding room to tell them that Lady Amanda would be coming. The manageress suggested they close the room to other mothers during her visit.

Joan firmly told her, "Lady Amanda would be horrified. She is the same as the other mothers."

At the station, Vincent and Holly impressed everyone with their questions and understanding they knew their parents explained to them how the police worked. Amanda showed her police expertise. The local policemen were so pleased she had come to see them. They all had drinks of fruit juice. Luca was happy in his pushchair.

Whilst Amanda and Joan went to the store feeding room, Mark took the triplets to the camera shop and Holly and Vincent went to look at the books in the store. They were thrilled to find a 'dress-up ballerina' book and a glitter sticker book with over one hundred sparkly stickers for Sophie, a giant animal-sticker colouring book and a junior sudoku book for Heather, and two sticker books of footballers and Horrid Henry for Eric. The manager was with them.

Vincent told him, "We are very pleased with your books, Mr Allen. These are perfect for our sisters and brother for their birthday."

Mr Allen was delighted. People – especially children – didn't often give them encouragement. He asked, "What do you think about the games?"

"We haven't had time to look," Holly told him, "but we will come another day, definitely before Christmas, to buy presents."

He thanked them. He shared their comments with the staff, who agreed what well-mannered, pleasant children they were.

On the way to the store Sophie had seen an outfit displayed in the windows of the shop next door.

"Daddy, will you buy me that please for my birthday?"

It was very cheap.

"We had better ask your mummy," Mark replied.

They went to find Amanda. She was talking animatedly with a group of mothers. A wave of love went through Mark. Amanda loved being in the community and she was natural with everyone.

When Joan saw Mark and the children were waiting, they said goodbye and Amanda greeted the manager and congratulated him on the feeding and toilet facilities. The store was crowded as it was a school holiday. The manager led them into the dining area. Everyone at the tables stood up out of respect and greeted them with smiles.

Sophie said, as she sipped her fruit juice, "I like it here."

They all agreed it was an unexpected pleasure. They enjoyed their sandwiches and cakes. Amanda promised the manager they would come again.

They went out and Mark told Amanda that Sophie wanted to look at an outfit in the shop next door. Amanda and Joan went in with her whilst the others waited outside. Some community police greeted Mark and peeped at Luca; they were looking out for Amanda. Passing police patrols waved.

After a short while Amanda, Joan and Sophie came out of the shop with bags of Sophie's birthday presents.

"I don't know what Jean will say," Amanda said.

"She will be able to copy them, Mummy," Sophie told her.

They all laughed.

Joan had bought two more birthday presents from her, Stan and Bob. She also bought two sparkly belts. They were having a fulfilling day getting the presents. Mark had bought Eric a new camera.

"Anywhere else?" Mark asked.

"May we go to the art shop, please, Daddy?" Heather asked.

Then they all took it in turns to go to the store toilets.

Mark and Amanda went into the arts-and-crafts shop with Heather, who asked for a set of pastel-coloured crayons for her birthday. Mark took her out whilst Amanda quickly bought a box of the latest Inktense, glue and glitter powders. Stan had fetched the 4 x 4; they all had an apple and then sang all the way home. The twins knew they would have DVDs and other presents, so they had asked their parents and the adults if they would please give them money.

"May Siobhan, Lauren and Trevor come to our birthday party, Mummy?" Sophie asked.

"Have you asked your brothers and sisters?"

"Yes, Mummy."

As their birthdays were all so close together they had a combined party. Amanda asked whom they would like to invite.

"The problem is, Mum, that if we invite some and not all, it will be showing favouritism," Eric told her.

Amanda never ceased to be amazed at their perception.

"We all would like Mr and Mrs Stewart and Auntie Muriel to come, with Granddad, Grandma, Uncle Josh and everyone. We all agreed this will be OK," Eric then told her.

"Oh, you have all discussed this?"

"Yes, Mum," he laughed.

She cuddled him. "You are very efficient," she teased. "Have you thought about Uncle Luca?"

"Yes, we must invite him. What about his grandchildren?"

"I think we had better invite them later, darling. Uncle Luca is in London just now. Now he has an apartment, the children are able to come with their mum and stay overnight. They could travel up on the express train."

"OK, Mum, let's do that. Are Auntie Sarah and Angela able to come?"

"They are coming, darling."

Eric and Sophie didn't know what to buy the twins. Heather had bought beakers with a design showing a mouse on a twig for Vincent and a butterfly for Eric. They asked them, and both Vincent and Holly asked for money to buy film for their cameras and photographic paper to print pictures on. They bought what they asked for and also bought them each a photograph album.

With the courts being closed, Lord Jonathan was flexible in

between attending meetings and lots of paperwork. He and Teresa delayed going to Italy until after the party.

As Amanda and Mark were soaking in the bath, she said, "I regret I cannot invite your mum and David to the party, darling. It would be too much for Dad, and I am not having him going off for the day whilst we are celebrating. He does live here."

"It is a mess, precious, but she didn't consider us when she was leaving."

"I know, darling. It still hurts, doesn't it?"

"Yes. The bottom of our world fell through. Dad was heartbroken. He felt guilty and full of regrets about neglecting her through pressure of work."

They both went quiet. In all these years Stan had never spoken to Amanda about this time. She hoped he would, but in no way would she interfere. During the four years she spent grieving for Andrew, she never spoke, even to her family, about how she was holding resentment and unforgiveness against Mark. She had kept her guilt and regrets to herself. She had loved Andrew, but, having known him since she was three years old, she hadn't been *in* love with him. They would have been happy in their marriage, and God willing they would have had children, but with his living for his antique cars and her passion for music and going to Italy for the operas there would always have been something missing in their relationship. Andrew had been to the Villa Verona with her, but she knew he was bored when they visited the opera. They didn't go again but spent the remaining few days walking or being with the Contessa. When she came to Chiverton and fell in love with Mark at first sight, she realised what had been missing with Andrew. She groaned.

"Anything wrong, precious?"

"No, my darling. I am not having your dad excluded. The children adore him. We will invite your mum and David another day. Come on, darling – time to get out. We will not mention this conversation."

He helped her out, and as he was washing her hair in the shower she was sobbing. He quickly rinsed it and held her until the storm had passed. They dried and put their robes on. She sat in her feeding chair and Mark brushed her hair. She loved having her hair washed and brushed.

"You have been far away, darling?"

"Yes, my precious, but I am back now."

She kissed him passionately. He could taste her tears.

Brenda quietly knocked on the door and Mark thanked her and took Luca to Amanda for his supper.

When Luca began on Chiverton home-produced solids Amanda's feeding routine changed accordingly, of course. Vincent, Holly and Eric had been, and still were, hearty eaters. Heather also had a good appetite, but Sophie was satisfied with small portions.

Gerald, as always, made the birthday cakes. Amanda and Mark asked the children what they would like to do after the party lunch. They all asked for a musical time and for Rose to dance if she would.

"Will you dance, darling?" Mark asked Sophie.

"No, Daddy, not with Rose being here. I will sing."

"OK, it is your birthday."

"Will you and Mummy sing, please?"

"Of course. Choose between you what songs you would like. Will you ask Granddad to play his violin?"

"Yes."

"Are you going to play your violin, Vincent? Your granddad and all of us would love to hear you."

"Yes, Dad, I will." (Vincent was getting quite professional through his lessons and practising.)

Mark told Amanda about Sophie not wishing to dance.

"I hope she doesn't feel intimidated by Rose," Amanda mused.

"Shall I have a word with her?" Mark asked.

"Yes please, darling."

He seized an opportunity and asked her, "Are you shy to dance in front of Rose, darling?"

"Oh no, Papa," – she often lapsed into calling him that – "I will be singing and I do not want to take attention from Rose."

He had to laugh. He cuddled her. "This is very gracious of you, pet," he said.

When he told Amanda, she laughed and said, "Wow! What can I say? Is she getting spoilt?"

"She is very beautiful, as you know, Amanda, and as she is also small she does attract attention. I cannot see any problems. Her brothers and sisters would soon deflate her; also Mrs Vine would let us know if there were any problems at school. Look how she is with Lauren and Siobhan."

"You are right as always, my darling. They are very God-blessed to have a father like you, as I am having you for my husband." She gathered him close and kissed him passionately.

When she met with the triplets she asked if they would ask their Aunt Muriel to sing and play.

Joshua's twins and Susan were staying for a week, but Rose was too busy with her ballet lessons to be able to spare so much time away from home; she was having extra lessons to prepare for her exams. Rose had bought Sophie the most beautiful book about ballet dancers with insights into their lives. She was thrilled.

Isabel had sent birthday presents and cards. In each card she had written that she was looking forward to seeing them before they went to Devon. The children didn't ask why Rose (she) wasn't coming. Mark and Amanda resolved to explain it to them when they were older.

Luca was sat in his highchair between Mark and Amanda. He was banging his spoon and making his happy noises. Anne had made him and Angela a fresh fruit jelly, and Mark gave him a spoonful with ice cream. He kept opening his mouth and banged his hands on his table when Mark didn't immediately feed him again. Everyone was laughing. When he had eaten it all, he looked disappointed.

Mark asked Amanda, "May he have a little more?"

"Yes. It will not hurt him."

However, when he had eaten this he looked at Mark in expectation.

"You have had enough for now, Luca," Mark told him.

He held his arms up. Mark lifted him out on to his knee and cuddled him.

Amanda had accompanied Jonathan playing his violin and the children had asked Mark to accompany their Uncle Luke on his saxophone and Uncle Adam on his guitar, playing 'When the Saints Go Marching In'. No one could keep still for this.

They all had a wonderful time. Jon, Sheila, Dennis and Yvonne had not heard Amanda and Mark sing before and they were enchanted. They realised how privileged they were to be welcomed into this family. Muriel played and sang.

They concluded with a community sing-song from words on the screen. Luke had filmed and Adam had taken photographs of the day, but these were not for general publication.

When the guests had left, Mark, Amanda and the children went for a swim and games. Amanda always used the indoor pool. After showering they had a bowl of chicken broth each and wholemeal bread and then went into the room the Queen had used, where, with unanimous agreement, they all watched a Harry Potter DVD Vincent had been given. They were allowed to stay up a little later than usual, but, exciting as the film was, they were all falling asleep before it ended.

As Mark walked from Brookwell Police Station with his PA to pick up the car one day a movement in a window caught his eye. A long tweed winter coat in Amanda's colours was being put on a stand. William (the PA) went for the car. The coat was lovely. The shopkeeper came to the door.

"This is Lady Amanda's size, sir. I have just unpacked it. We have several items that were ordered, but the business has gone bankrupt. It is beautifully made – lovely with boots or shoes."

"Yes."

"Would you like to take it for Lady Amanda to try?"

"Is that fair?"

"Of course, sir. I wouldn't let just anyone, but I can make an exception for Lady Amanda. As it is out of season, it is half price."

"How much?"

She told him.

He thought, 'No wonder they have gone bankrupt!' Then he thought, 'If it costs this much half price, it must be good.'

"Yes, I will take it," he said. "Do you want me to pay now?"

"No, Chief Constable, seeing as it is you." She laughed.

He was still standing outside the shop when William arrived with the car. The owner passed him the bag.

Mark laughed to himself. "What will Amanda say to me buying her a winter coat when it is so hot?"

When he arrived home he took it up to their room. Amanda was with the children as usual. He quickly showered and changed into casuals. When he and Amanda met upstairs before dinner, he gave her the bag and she lifted the coat out.

"This is gorgeous, Mark. Have you bought it?"

He told her how it came about and said he would pay on the following day if it fitted.

She hurriedly tried it on. It fitted perfectly. She loved it.

"This must have cost the earth!"

"Well, nearly." He wasn't going to spoil it by telling her it was half price.

He put it back in the cover and hung it up.

She took him in her arms and kissed him. "You are always surprising me, darling," she said.

Amanda told the family during dinner, "My husband has bought me a beautiful tweed winter coat. It fits perfectly."

They all laughed. A winter coat in the summer!

When Amanda showed Jean, she told her it was beautiful and she couldn't have made it for the price.

"It must have been very expensive, Jean."

"Yes, but it was part of some bankrupt stock they were selling at half price."

"Half price!" echoed Amanda. She started laughing. "My husband didn't tell me that."

"Oh, I am sorry, ma'am. I shouldn't have said. Susan told me when I was looking in the window."

"That's all right, Jean; we will not let on."

They both laughed.

Amanda told Joan, Stan and Bob at lunch about her coat being half price and Mark not revealing that. She asked if they would tease him by bringing into their dinner conversation that they had seen or bought something at half price. Stan promised to let Luke and Adam in on the joke.

It began that evening with Stan, next Luke, next Adam, then Bob, then Joan. Mark didn't react in any way.

Amanda thought, 'He is using his training.'

After a week they gave up.

A few evenings later, Mark said, "You mentioned bargains you had seen or bought at half price; well, I have a confession to make."

They waited.

"I bought Amanda's winter coat at half price because the shop went bankrupt."

Amanda in serious mode said, "Oh, Mark, I wouldn't have known! It is such a beauty!"

They all went quiet, wondering what to say next, when Mark started laughing. "Gotcha!" he said.

They all collapsed with laughter.

Owing to the recession, new cars were not being made at the factory, but orders still poured in for parts to restore cars. There was a great demand from garages and private owners. Sergio Rossi's friend Signor Saracino, who had bought his and Luca's ships, enquired if they could make some parts for him. Simon and John went on the Eurostar train to Italy to find out their requirements. They brought back diagrams, and Signor Saracino sent samples. Fortunately they were able to produce these parts on the new machines. There was rejoicing in the local area about this new work to supply all the ships in Signor Saracino's fleet in turn. Amanda invited Tony, Simon, John and Gavin to lunch to celebrate this. Double shifts had to continue, and when two more old machines were updated two more mechanics were employed.

"It would be brilliant if you could come again to the factory and meet the new workers, Amanda," Adam said.

"Yes, I would love to come again. I promised I would not be remote."

Her visit was set up for that Wednesday morning, and Stan, Bob, and Joan to look after Luca, went with her. The afternoon shift workers came in to meet her again. The visit was a great success. They all appreciated her coming. They recognised her intelligence and noticed that she listened carefully while Simon and John were speaking. They told her they were very relieved her husband was the new Chief Constable, and they presented Amanda with a bouquet of rosebuds.

Natalie, Adam's PA, took Amanda and Joan into his office, where Amanda fed Luca in privacy. Then Simon, Gavin and John joined them with Adam. Natalie and Robin brought trays of pots of tea, sandwiches and cakes.

"These pots are gorgeous," she told them.

Natalie shyly told her, "We know you like sweet peas, ma'am, but we were unable to get a set with a sweet-pea design. Mr Young said you would like this pattern."

She warmly thanked them and they all tucked in. She thanked them again for their welcome. "My children and husband, with Mr Dansie and his family, will come during the school holiday."

They were all very pleased about this and word spread round the shop floor and the packing room.

During the second week in July, Mrs Burton had sent a notice to the local college (as she had every year the last seven years) asking for six trainee chefs specialising in preserving to apply by letter with references and health checks to Chiverton Manor. She also advertised for help with picking fruit in the first week in August. Students from the universities applied as before. Those with the best references were chosen, and Mrs Brown, the local Women's Institute food-preservation expert, had promised to come again. Everyone, including the children at Chiverton, helped to pick the fruits.

The preserving room was three steps down from the kitchen. It had a floor of stone flags and granite benches. It was cool but dry and well ventilated. Everything stayed in tip-top condition. Six years previously Amanda had bought an extra-massive deep freeze.

Mrs Burton had to buy more and more special preserving jars each year as the fruit grew in more and more abundance in the orchard. The number of peaches, nectarines and the other fruits growing on the south-facing wall had also increased. The first year the family had tasted the peaches they were so gorgeous that they made pigs of themselves! Nothing was wasted. The produce was frozen, stored, bottled or made into chutneys, jams and jellies. Grapefruits were made into marmalade; soups were made and frozen; vegetables were also frozen. Bob and Stan made perry.

It was a mammoth operation. The children were not allowed into the kitchen and preserving room, where there was an electric six-ring cooker. Muriel came for two days and helped. In the afternoons she and Amanda gave the children their piano lesson, then they went for a swim. Mrs Shulot enjoyed herself washing up and cleaning. Amanda always shared the harvest with her.

Chapter 20

"There's a new hygienist at the dentist," Adam mentioned casually at dinner. "She is coming to the gym this evening."

Amanda several times had invited him and Luke to bring their girlfriends to Chiverton Manor. They always thanked her but both said, "I need to know whether they are interested in me or coming here."

Amanda understood.

At breakfast the following morning, Mark asked innocently, "Did the hygienist come?"

"Yes, she is in good shape – she lifts weights and everything."

He and Amanda knew he would keep them posted.

A few mornings later Adam asked, "Amanda, is it OK for me to eat out this evening?"

"Of course, darling. I will let Gerald know."

They all waited, but he didn't say anything further. He often ate out after that. This continued for a month. He then told them, "Janette is a Christian; she would like to go to The Open Church on Sunday morning."

Amanda waited.

"Do you think she could come back for lunch, please, Amanda?"

"She will be very welcome, Adam. What would she like to eat?"

"Whatever we have, Amanda, thank you."

They were all pleased he was secure enough with this girl to invite her; this was a first.

"We'll all have to give our teeth a special clean," Luke teased him. He had seen Janette at the gym. She was quite something!

That Sunday it was a glorious morning. When it was almost time

149

for them to come, Amanda, Mark and the children went upstairs. Amanda gave Luca a 'top-up'. He was now on Chiverton-grown, cooked solids.

The Reverend Matthew was visiting his parents in Scotland; the Seddons family couldn't come because the children had measles. It was going around.

The dogs began barking and raced to the gate as the cars came in. Adam brought Janette to introduce her.

Amanda and Janette took to each other immediately. She was so natural, and the children loved her on sight, as did all the family.

It was a very relaxed lunch. They drank their spring water, which Janette said was gorgeous. She had a wonderful sense of humour. Luca was in his chair, kicking his legs and arms about. Mark fed him and they all laughed as he opened his mouth before Mark managed to get the spoon to him.

Sophie asked, "Janette, are you going to marry Uncle Adam."

Everyone went quiet.

Janette laughed. "Well, Sophie, (a) he hasn't asked me yet, and (b) I am returning to university for at least another four years. Then I will be a proper dentist and I will be able to pull your teeth out."

They all laughed.

Mark was thinking, 'Well done!'

They recognised that she came from a good family. She had a beautiful voice.

"We are all cleaning our teeth extra-hard now, Janette," Eric told her.

"That's good, Eric. You have wonderful teeth."

Amanda asked if she and her parents were settled in this area.

"Yes, thank you, ma'am. We like it very much. The practice in Chesterton is a very busy one; I am pleased I am able to help my parents whilst I am on holiday."

Adam then told them, "Janette has two older brothers: one is a dentist and the other is a GP."

Luke mentioned the text that the Reverend Standall had preached on.

"It was very interesting," Janette said. "I thought he explained it very well for the people who came for the thanksgiving of the baby. They are obviously not regular churchgoers."

Between them, Adam, Luke and Janette briefly told Amanda and Mark about it. They realised that she knew the Bible well.

They had almost finished the meal when Mark's secure mobile rang. He asked to be excused and listened.

"I'm sorry, darling," he said, turning to Amanda. "The Divisional Commander and my deputy are coming to see me on urgent business.

She knew it must be important. Although Mark was on call every evening until 10 p.m., this was the first time they had contacted him on his secure mobile.

"Please finish your meal," Mark said to the others.

The car arrived and Amanda kissed him. "Be as quick as possible," she said.

He promised that he would.

"I understand, darling," Amanda replied.

She went with him to greet his colleagues and asked them if they would like a drink or anything?

"We would appreciate a coffee, ma'am."

They went to Mark's private office and Amanda rang Mrs Burton to arrange the coffee. She went back and settled down with the others and they ate their apple and cheese.

"I'll stay with you this afternoon," Joan told Amanda.

Stan echoed that.

"No, darlings. Please go to the cricket as you have arranged. It's a beautiful afternoon and your friends will be disappointed if you do not go."

"Will you please swim with us, Uncle Luke?" Vincent asked.

"Yes, if your mum agrees."

"Please do, Luke."

"We'll use the outdoor pool."

Amanda looked at Janette.

"I would love to swim with them, ma'am. May I fetch my costume?"

"There are new costumes ready for such times as this, Janette. Please help yourself."

"Are you free to come with us, Lady Amanda?"

"I will attend to Luca and wait for my husband, but thank you."

Sandra brought two costumes for Janette to choose from.

They went outside and had a stroll until their meal was digested. Sophie and Heather were holding Janette's hands; then the children went upstairs with Amanda to change. Adam took Janette to the outdoor-pool changing rooms.

Sally had Sundays off until 7 p.m. when she came to attend to Luca. When Amanda had changed him and given him his 'top-up', she took him back down in his pram to the outside table, where she typed into her laptop more of the story she was writing about Sparky. Luca was sound asleep.

Mark came to find her. His colleagues had gone through the side door so as not to disturb them.

"I need to do some work on my laptop, darling," he said. "I'll put you in the picture later, when we won't be interrupted."

They both sat typing away until the three girls came running to them. Heather's hair was loose, and she told them, "Janette has washed our hair; Mummy, we have had a good time."

Holly and Sophie smilingly agreed. Mark and Amanda cuddled them. Vincent and Eric came with Luke, Adam and Janette, all smiling, saying how they had enjoyed it. Amanda thanked Janette for helping the girls.

"May we have a game of football now, Dad?" Eric asked. "If that is what you have decided, please excuse me. I have some work to type in. I will be as quick as I can."

Sophie stayed with her parents after she had fetched her dressing-up dolls. The others were all obviously enjoying the football, judging by the noise they were making. Amanda and Mark smiled at each other.

Later they all settled at the tables for fruit drinks and tea. Adam went to Janette's for tea before going to the lively local Fellowship church evening service.

When Mark had finished his work, he went with Amanda in her chair and Luca, who had now woken up, in his pushchair for a walk in the wood with the dogs. The children were doing their homework.

They returned for 5.30 Sunday supper. Luke ate with them

before going to the Methodist church for the worship service. He was now part of the Methodist worship group, and he was a respected member of their fellowship, but they understood his commitment with The Open Church.

During dinner Stan told them it had been an enjoyable cricket match, although the other team had won.

Amanda told them about the swim and laughingly told him, "She washed the girl's hair and then they all played football."

They all agreed that Janette appeared to be a very nice young lady – probably a bit of a tomboy. "Yes, with two older brothers, that's very likely," Stan said.

"It must be serious for Adam to bring her home," Bob mused.

"It's early days yet," Stan said. "She will be at Oxford for several more years. If it is God's will, they will continue – I do pray so."

Stan, Bob, Joan and Mrs Burton went back to talking about the cricket.

As they were soaking in the bath, Mark told Amanda about the case he was now on.

"We will need to work from here for a few days, darling. We will use the side door; my colleagues will be coming and going."

"Let me know if you need anything, sweetheart," Amanda replied.

Mark and his colleagues came often to his private office. They worked through their lunch break and brought their own sandwiches. Mrs Burton provided spring water, fruit and coffee.

Chapter 21

In the last week in August the family went to join Nicola and Joshua in Devon. Amanda asked Adam if Janette would like to come with them.

"Thank you, Amanda, but it would be too much of a statement. We do enjoy each other's company, but I am concentrating on my job and Janette is going back to university for at least four years. We are going to keep in touch and there are the holidays."

"This is very mature of you, Adam. I am very proud of my younger brother."

He blushed and laughed.

The weather forecast wasn't good, but they could all find something to do. Stan, Bob and Joan could go golfing; Luke and Adam surfing. The children packed DVDs, games and quizzes and they could swim in the indoor pool or play football and other games. They had left kites at Seaways when they were there in May.

As Joshua said, "The kids are never at a loss."

Brenda would sleep in the mornings then go out with Anne and Jayne. They had the afternoons off.

Sophie couldn't wait to get to the draper's shop. She had saved her birthday money and pocket money to buy things she could share with Siobhan and Lauren. As promised, Mrs Oliver had saved oddments of glitter gems, sequin patches, various transparent glass shapes, glass jewels and acrylic jewels. The dressmakers had set aside any leftover materials covered in rhinestones and coloured sequins. Sophie was thrilled; these were different to what she had bought at home.

"I will share these with my two new friends," she said.

Mrs Oliver had also saved pieces of ribbon and braid and small pieces of material and dried flowers for Heather to use on her cards.

She told Amanda and Nicola that they had some pure wool challis in with a sparkly thread running through.

"Mum hasn't mentioned these," Nicola said.

"We have rushed them through, madam, in preparation for you coming," Mrs Oliver told her.

She led them to the rolls; they were in gorgeous colours and a variety of weights. Naturally Sophie loved them, and so did Heather.

"Rose will like these, Mum," Susan suggested.

"Yes, she will. What about you, darling?"

"I wouldn't mind a jacket, please."

"Have you patterns, Mrs Oliver?"

"Yes, madam." They brought the pattern books and Mrs Oliver suggested, "If you haven't time to look through them in the shop, you are welcome to take them with you. I know you will return them quickly."

Amanda and Nicola thanked her. Amanda was looking at a pink, green and gold square tweed with a gold thread running through. "I would like a two-piece in this, Nicci. I have the pattern you gave me."

They all agreed that the colour would suit her.

The assistant brought a pattern. Amanda and Nicola liked the style. Amanda bought it. They promised to return the next morning.

Amanda bought materials for the polyester, elastane and transparent voile evening dress in amethyst blue, as well as materials for winter clothes for the children, including Luca and Joan. Joan ordered cones of wool to knit on her machine, as well as double-knitting wool for her to knit thicker clothes by hand and more angora. She and Mrs Burton had also brought wool from home, but Mrs Oliver and staff made them all so welcome that they were keen to support the shop.

As Amanda was going into the private room to feed Luca, Mrs Oliver asked if they would like a pot of tea. They welcomed this, and when she rejoined them Susan, Heather and Sophie were having glasses of fruit juice.

The men and the other children went to the shop which had been selling bankrupt stock, but they were very disappointed to find it had closed.

There were two new, very popular films on at the four-screen cinema, and they asked Amanda and Nicola if they could go to see one of them the next day. It wasn't as yet booked up. Sophie and Heather asked if they could go too. They were satisfied with their purchases. The forecast was for rain. After a short discussion, Amanda and Nicola decided they would go to the draper's in a hired car to choose materials whilst the others all went to the cinema.

Stan, Bob, Vincent and Eric went back to book seats. The others all caught the bus back to Seaways. Stan and Bob, laughing, called at the draper's to tell Mrs Oliver that Mrs Young and Mrs Dansie would be coming to the shop on the following afternoon.

The cinema visit was such a success that Joshua booked them all in to see another popular film. They all went, leaving Amanda and Mark to have the afternoon on their own whilst Luca slept.

They discussed what they would do to complete their holiday, and Stan suggested an afternoon coach ride round the coast. He pointed out that the coach stopped at a hotel where baby-feeding facilities were available. The hotel also provided afternoon tea. They all voted for this, and Stan booked it and the afternoon tea. It was his and Bob's treat, as had been the cinema visit. Stan arranged for the small coach to pick them up; they almost filled it!

Amanda and Mark had, with approval, booked Joshua and Nicola for lunch at the hotel where they were friends of the owners.

Joshua asked, "Aren't you both coming with us? I thought that is what we decided."

"Yes, darling, we did discuss it, but we want you and Nicci to have time alone."

"Fair enough, sis. Thank you."

Joshua had hired a car and when he and Nicola were ready to leave they both looked devastating. Joshua wore a pale-grey suit with a black silk open-neck shirt, and Nicola wore a glamorous dress. The others all told them so and took photographs of them in different poses.

The coach trip scenery was fantastic. The children were taking photographs and Luke was filming. The hotel was first class, and they all tucked into the sandwiches and cakes. Luca in his highchair enjoyed the Cornish ice cream, as all the children did. It wasn't warm enough for them to sit outside, but before they left they promised they would return in the following May.

When the men at the allotment were first told that Mark had sown his sweet-pea seeds, they were laughing.

"He'll not get long, strong, straight stalks with that peat-free rubbish he uses," one of them declared.

The following July Mark showed the men his sweet peas and asked them if they were good enough to show at Chatsworth. When they saw them, they didn't scoff about peat-free compost again!

"Will you be entering, sir?" Mick asked.

"No, I have decided not to this year after all."

They were relieved.

This visit of the men from the allotment became a yearly event. The men always brought sweet peas and other flowers for Amanda and fruit for the children. Amanda always had plenty of sandwiches and cakes made for them. As they came on foot Mark supplied them with glasses of beer. They all enjoyed these afternoons. Amanda and the children took photographs to give them, and the men were proud to show these to their families and friends.

Mark took the children to their allotments, but Amanda couldn't manage to get there. The paths were too rough for her, either walking or in her chair.

Every September the children and Amanda filled plant pots with the peat-free compost for Mark's seeds, which he soaked overnight before sowing. They left them to overwinter in a cold frame.

As promised, when the children returned to school in September they brought a few of the photographs to pass round their classes. Sophie, as expected, told her class about the portrait of her parents. Eric and Heather said how beautiful it was and mentioned that they would be going to Sandringham for the second week in January.

Eric told them, "It's flat there for my mummy. Balmoral is too hilly."

Chapter 22

The Queen, Prince Philip and Princess Anne came to Chiverton again on Friday 24 September. The Duke and Duchess also came. It was just a short visit as the Queen was entertaining VIPs from France for the weekend. No one else was invited. It was a beautiful mellow autumn day – the trees were turning colour. When the Queen got out of the helicopter she was laughing.

"I am getting more used to these helicopters," she said.

In the hall they looked at the portrait they had given Amanda and the new one of Mark in his chief-constable uniform. Amanda told them the children were having their portrait also painted to symbolise continuation.

The upstairs routine was worked through as before. They all enjoyed their relaxed lunch. Princess Anne asked Amanda about the factory, and she told them about the ships, the ongoing orders from the Italian airline, and that they were having two apprentices trained at the local college.

"We had a problem: a young lady applied," Amanda told her. · They laughed.

Princess Anne said, "Good for her! I hope you employed her."

"Yes, ma'am, we did."

After coffee they went into the sunshine for the Queen to see the gardens. Prince Philip couldn't wait to see the Bugatti. Princess Anne, as she had requested, went with the children to see their ponies.

The Prince passed them, driving the Bugatti with Stan at his side. He looked so happy. The Queen was laughing. He invited her to get in, but she laughingly declined. Luke was filming and the children were taking photographs for their personal albums. Adam went back to work.

Amanda and Mark showed the Queen the gardens and greenhouses. Sophie was holding her hand. The Queen was laughing at what Sophie was telling her.

Mark thought, 'I hope she isn't asking the Queen if she has any sparklies!'

The Queen was very interested in everything and she asked Nigel a lot of questions.

Mark told her, "We recycle all our waste water for the gardens and greenhouses – also, when necessary, for the sprinklers for the grass, ma'am, and all the waste."

She laughed at this. "I must tell Prince Charles. He will want to come to discuss this."

A mist was falling – the promise of a beautiful day tomorrow – as they set off in gumboots to walk down to the river with all the dogs. The dogs, as usual, swam and chased about. There was the scent of woodsmoke in the air, and autumn smells from the damp earth. Princess Anne went past driving the Bugatti with her dad at her side. They looked so relaxed and carefree.

They returned for afternoon tea – this time in the sitting room. Vincent was telling the Queen about the schools designing Christmas cards and where the money had gone. She listened intently and asked what the next project would be. Holly told her they were designing Easter cards. She was surprised.

"Easter?"

"Yes, ma'am, the cards have to prepared months in advance."

All too soon it was time for the royal family to leave. It was dusk. The Queen said that they were looking forward to them coming to Sandringham in January; then they said their goodbyes and the helicopter set off. They stood waving until it was out of sight.

"When they come next spring, I am positive they will fly their kites," said Vincent.

"Yes, more than likely!" laughed Amanda.

When the Duke and Duchess had left, Amanda and Mark went swimming with the children, full of joy because everyone had enjoyed themselves so much.

The children had some brilliant photographs of Prince Philip and Princess Anne driving the Bugatti. Luke sent these with the film.

On the eve of Luca's first birthday, Amanda and Mark were having their usual soak and Mark was massaging Amanda's leg (the therapy was ongoing). They all knew her leg would never be perfect, but the muscles and ligaments were slowly healing and she was thankful that it wasn't as painful as it had been.

She said, "Mark, sweetheart?"

"Ye-es?" (He knew what was coming!)

"I am strong, and everything is in working order; you are at your peak."

"Ye-es?"

"Well, do you think we could try?"

"Yes – I expected this."

Amanda had a comfortable pregnancy. The scan showed twins; they again did not ask the sexes. They were as active and healthy as her other babies.

On 2nd December healthy twin boys each weighing just over 4 kilos were delivered without any problem. There was great rejoicing, they were both fair-haired and both had a strong resemblance to Mark.

Mark asked Amanda, "Are you satisfied now?"

"We-ell," she teased, "–thank you, yes."